Storyteller

THREE /// OWLS
PUBLISHING

EDITORS
Lydia Silbernagel
Shay Shivecharan

COVER
Photographer: Jeannie Albers
Model: Blake Slaughter

 storytellermag.com

 info@storytellermag.com

 fb.com/storytellermagazine

 @storytellermagazine

---

Storyteller is a quarterly publication that celebrates truth through writing. In its pages, you will find poetry, fiction, and nonfiction, each piece an expression of truth as known or experienced by its creator.

JEANNIE ALBERS

jalbersstudio.com | jeannie@jalbersstudio.com

PORTRAIT - COMMERCIAL - STUDIO & LOCATION - LIFESTYLE - FASHION

POETRY

Today, Everywhere I've Gone   13
by Seth Kaye

Like the Sun   14
by Londyn Rayne

Binge Sinner   15
by Tanner Johns

The Difference Between Shadows and Silhouettes   32
by Blake Slaughter

An Excerpt, from Rain this Afternoon   64
by Seth Kaye

Sunrise   65
by Cole Reeves

FICTION

Insomnibus   6
by Aaron Morrison

The Magical Miniature Golf Course of Poblano Beach   16
by Clay Waters

Pinballs   36
by Larry Griffin

The House Always Wins   66
by Cooper Nickerson

She Who Burns   79
by Gabriel McLeod

A Few Feet from Normalcy   99
by Joshua Mahn

Authors

Cooper Nickerson

My name is Cooper Nickerson and I am 61 year old deaf man. I was born in Wood's Harbour, Nova Scotia, Canada. I am currently residing in Waterloo, Ontario. I studied at St Mary's University, 1981-1983. I work as a siding and window installer. My sporting passion is duck hunting. In my spare time, I write short stories and read a lot of books. I have three boys, a daughter and three granddaughters.

Blake Slaughter @blakeeslaughter

Blake Slaughter, born in Orlando and raised in Clermont, Florida, has had a passion for writing since he was eleven. Envisioning stories of horror and drama, he took up writing and hasn't stopped. He attributes a lot of his inspiration to music- from Frank Sinatra to Led Zeppelin. Other inspirations include authors Stephen King and William Peter Blatty, poets Edgar Allen Poe and Walt Whitman- most notably his poem "I Sing the Body Electric", and the American film director Stanley Kubrick.

Londyn Rayne @londynrayne

Londyn Rayne is a songwriter, lyricist, music producer, and a performing member in the band Sunset Roulett. She is also the founder of Orlando based ministry Label Me His. An advocate for mental/emotional health and healing, Londyn finds comfort in connecting with the power of words and expressing her pain and passions creatively whether it be through music, poetry or photography. She is soon releasing her first poetry collection and believes vulnerability is the beautiful beginning of transformation.

Aaron Morrison @theaaronmorrison

Aaron was born during the great ________natural disaster__________ in the ____season____ of ____year____. He spends his free time exploring _________unusual location_________ and raising domesticated ________ fictional creature(plural)_________. One day, he would like to _____verb_____ his way to _______place_______ and try the various _____noun(plural)_____.

Larry Griffin @flightofgriffin

Larry Griffin was born in Orlando and raised on a steady diet of horror movies and books, which has contributed to his writing, along with much attention paid to the state of the world today. In his free time, he can be found at the movie theater or the beach. He's had stories published in Bards and Sages Society of Misfit Stories, Hellbound Books and other local and online publications. He's also had journalism published in numerous papers and magazines.

Cole Reeves @nicholasmichaelreeves

Nicholas "Cole" Reeves, 23, does not like the word writer, but does love to write. His heroes are Billy Collins, Gregory Alan Isakov, Ray Bradbury, Le Petit Prince, and of course, his mother. In 2018, he graduated from Stetson University with a degree in finance. He currently works at Lockheed Martin in Orlando, FL, on the Javelin missile, but poetry is his true love. He has a book club in Winter Garden, called The Paper Cuts. You can reach him at nmreeves2@gmail.com if you'd like to join the party.

Authors

Clay Waters

Clay Waters lived in Florida until the age of four and recently returned to find it hasn't changed a bit. Three of his six memories from that first stop involve the alphabet in some form, which in retrospect was a bit of a tell. He has had stories published in *The Santa Barbara Review*, *Abyss & Apex*, and *Morpheus Tales*, and has self-published a "cozy," English-country-house whodunnit?, *Death in the Eye*.

Joshua Mahn @joshmahnwrites

Joshua Mahn is made manifest by the shared belief in his existence. While you may never be certain if other folks around you are real, it can be guaranteed that Joshua Mahn, most certainly, is not.

He would also like to say that, for a small donation of fresh seal flesh or dried caribou meat, he will rid your house of all copper wiring, setting you free from the tethers of modern convenience.

Tanner Johns

Tanner Johns bartends in order to fund his goal to become the first tree-hugger to hug a tree on Mars. Wish him luck with that. He's afraid of heights. When he's not bartending, he's writing, drawing, reading about space, playing video games, or sleeping. Usually all at the same time. He's a cool guy.

Seth Kaye @iamsethkaye

Seth Kaye is learning to be a poet. Though predisposed to the misconception that poetry is either world-alteringly legendary or utterly worthless (with no space in between), he has tasked himself with cultivating the elusive terrain in the middle. Devoted to the art of songwriting, Seth has only recently allowed himself to indulge in the writing of poems sans musical accompaniment. Fueled by a passion for language and the lyrical expression of human experience and emotion, he is on his way.

Gabriel McLeod @gabrielmcleod

Gabriel McLeod hails from a southern town intersected by railroads and rivers, canopied by magnolia and moonlight. He was born from a family of hard workers, dreamers and storytellers. He currently is working on a collection of short stories, a book of poetry and the beginning stages of a novel. Gabriel made Orlando his home for over 20 years and proudly lives with two extraordinary daughters and two enigmatic cats in a house with full bookshelves in every room.

Storyteller is always looking for new voices and fresh perspectives. Submissions can be made to: **storytellersubmissions@gmail.com**

INSOMNIBUS

BY AARON MORRISON

I've always felt excitement and nervousness

before a band goes on. The energy from the crowd. A subconscious worry the band will suck live. The anticipation of hearing and experiencing versions of songs that will only exist in that moment. The attitude and presence of the band itself. That shared experience that can never truly be captured or understood unless you were there.

My anxiety is always enhanced by my own dislike of crowds which, I suppose, stands in strong contention with my personal love of seeing live music. One of the reasons I tend to stand on the outer edges of the crowd, and almost never in it.

Tonight held more anticipation than usual. Insomnibus rarely toured, given the group had disbanded roughly twenty years ago, after releasing only two albums. Those two albums, however, were highly influential in the genre, and the bassist, Cal, and guitarist, Mike, had gone on to front two other bands that were highly successful, in their own right. They would occasionally get together to record and release a song or two under their original moniker, but it wasn't until last year that they finally released a new full album.

I realize that this, while a perfectly valid reason, seems quite mundane in comparison to my level of excited expectancy. My anticipation had been enhanced by all the research I had done. To be clear, the rabbit hole I went down was not some "super fan" obsession to know all the little details of the band. I had noticed in Insomnibus's lyrical content, cover art, and general vibe, a possible connection to something beyond music. Through these various interconnecting threads of knowledge, and my own esoteric education, I had come to a conclusion that, to anyone outside of the situation, would find insane or laughable. But I was certain, well, almost certain, of my findings.

I had grown up in the era of "satanic panic" in music. Bands putting blatant satanic and occult imagery on their album art, even if all they sang about were motorcycles and strippers. Other bands wrote lyrics that contained, from implied to explicit, references to the occult and devil worship, to varying degrees of seriousness. There were several high profile cases where certain bands' music seemed to be rooted in the "cause" of some horrific events. The added influence of drugs, mental illness, the perpetrator wanting an excuse, and the public wanting a reason and something to blame, muddied just how direct the correlation of the music to violent acts was.

The debate on how much various forms of art influences culture, and vice versa, has always raged on. I won't engage in a full debate here, but some level of influence, music in particular, is undeniable.

It was through my own research of the occult that had led me to make the connections that I did. I had found those branching threads that guided me into the darker, and mostly forgotten corners, of hidden knowledge. The existence of ancient upon ancient beings that ruled as gods throughout our universe. Many had held sway over our planet until they were driven into hiding, or had been banished to other planes. As my knowledge of these things grew, I began to see the web that was laced across and through our existence. It was a burden I had not been prepared for, but it was now mine. Once that veil has been lifted, it is impossible to put it back in place.

It would be dishonest of me to say there wasn't at least a nugget of doubt in my mind. It could very well be that Insomnibus had simply liked the imagery that this hidden world of knowledge invoked. But the references, as well as the timing of releases, showed a much more deliberate and specific employment of said knowledge. Again, I could have been wrong, and this was just another case of a band using imagery because it was "cool" or an attention seeking publicity stunt, but the subtlety in their presentation did not line up right if that's all it was. It might not have even been intentional. It wouldn't be farfetched to assume that some bands, or anyone for that matter, would become unwitting pawns in a game they did not understand. Regardless, if I was wrong, the worst that could happen would be that I would enjoy a good show. But, if

I was right...

My thoughts were broken as an audio sample from some forgotten movie that was used on the new album played through the speakers. The rhythmic thud of the bass drum soon followed. The heavy distortion of the guitar filled in an in time, but seemingly disjointed, riff. The bass started to add the same. Eight strikes down on the toms and all three instruments unified in a thunderous and mighty wave.

I allowed the music to sweep over me and let the visions it invoked become clear in my mind. As my body swayed, and my head nodded with the rhythm of the music, my consciousness began to slip into another time. I could see the ancient ziggurats that stood as monuments and places of worship for the ancient gods that once ruled this planet. High above the tops of the massive structures, winged beasts circled. Their grey flesh blotted with dark green patches not unlike the moss and kudzu encased corners of the ziggurats. Hideous humanoid beings ungelated

> **" I could see the ancient ziggurats that stood as monuments and places of worship for the ancient gods that once ruled this planet.**

and worshiped at the bases. The grotesque half spawn of man and the twisted offspring servants of the god they called out to.

My vision pulled back, and I was again fully aware of my surroundings. I opened my eyes, which were now adjusted to the relative dark of the concert venue. I looked to my right, catching the eye of the attractive bartender, who smiled sweetly. If I hadn't had my current task at hand, and if I was a braver man, I would have spoken to her. Instead, I smiled softly back, sheepishly averted my gaze, and scanned the crowd.

I saw what I was looking for. There were only three, but there, interspersed among the concert goers, were the same spawn I had seen in my vision. The music was calling them up. I knew what I had to do now.

I kept a balance of resolve of intent and experience of the music. I perhaps did not enjoy the concert as fully as I would have, but the quality of music was undeniable.

The concert eventually ended, and I made my way outside. I walked to the side of the venue, hands in my pockets, head down, shoulders hunched, as it was lightly raining. I crossed the street, and turned down an alleyway that ran between two buildings across from the venue. I stood under what awning I could find, lit a cigarette and waited. The smell from the dumpster, graciously, wasn't unbearable, and the smoke from the cigarette helped block that sweet and sick smell of rot. I wasn't sure how long I would need to wait, but I would as long as was necessary.

I sensed the presence of my quarry before I saw him. One of the people I had seen shift into the creatures during the concert was ambling across the street and turned down the alleyway between the concert venue and the building next door. I took one last drag off the current cigarette I was smoking, before dropping it on the wet ground. This hiss was soon extinguished, as was the cigarette, after I put the ball of my foot to it. Thankfully, the crowd had fully dispersed so no one watched me as I briskly walked across the street and followed the half spawn into the alley.

I carefully, and quietly, began preparing a spell. I did not want to draw too much power too quickly, not wanting my target to become aware of the changes in energy before I was ready to deal with the creature on my terms. I was, admittedly, highly inexperienced in my current endeavor. My studies in magic, and the harnessing of said power, had been mostly theoretical, and certainly nothing to the extent at which I was about to enact. My thoughts were quickly flooded with all the ways this could go sideways and how I was probably in over my head. Those thoughts were interrupted when I sensed some new and powerful energy. At the end of the alley the half spawn and I had been walking down, appeared the guitarist of the band. Mike's tattoos glowed bright gold as he summoned in energy. The half spawn, now shifting between its human and true creature form, turned around and ran. I reacted as quickly as I could, clumsily finishing the spell. A ball of sparking neon pink energy lept from my hands like the minor flames of a gas station firework. The creature lashed out with one of its flailing limbs, knocking me back as it ran past. I fell back, painfully falling on my ass, but gaining some comfort in seeing my spell had enough power behind it to slightly trip up the half spawn. I was getting myself up off the wet ground as Mike ran past, giving chase, huffing and puffing, clearly out of shape. The creature was nearing the entrance of the alley when Cal stepped out, blocking the exit. He waved his arms in front of him in a circular motion, summoning forth a large circular shield-like manifestation of deep purple energy. Cal pushed the shield forward, helping it meet the half spawn that was running full speed. The impact knocked the creature flat on its back, which allowed Mike to catch up. The gold energy flowed fully into his hand, which he brought down onto the creature's chest. The half spawn glowed briefly before dissipating in a cloud of particles in a strange, silent poof.

Mike had his hands on his knees, still catching his breath. "What is it they always say in the movies? 'I'm getting too old for this shit?'" Mike pointed to himself. "I feel that. That's me."

Cal chuckled. He nodded and gestured towards me as I approached.

Mike turned around. "Thanks for the assist."

"Yeah. No problem. I mean, I don't know how much I helped, but, yeah."

"First time?"

I nodded.

"It gets easier. Sort of. I don't fuckin' know."

"We should probably get out of here." Cal looked around to make sure no one had witnessed what happened.

Mike nodded in agreement and motioned for me to follow them. We made our way to their tour bus, which Cal entered and Mike sat down on the step of the entrance. Mike lit up a joint, took a toke, and handed it to me. Feeling it would have been rude to refuse, I accepted, took a toke myself, then handed it back.

"Helps calm the nerves after all that. The energy you use takes a fuckin' toll after a while."

"How long you been...?" I gestured with my head back to the alley.

"Twenty-five years now? Long story short, we started seeing the reality of what was going on. Barriers between the worlds getting thin. Shit like that. Figured we'd do what we could to, I dunno, hold back the flood. Kind of feels like that whole Dutch kid sticking his fingers in the fucking dam or whatever, but..." Mike shrugged.

Cal appeared at the doorway of the tour bus. He tossed a book to me.

The book looked old, bound in some kind of leather, with strange runes on the cover.

"That helped us." Cal said. "Should help you too."

"Thanks," I responded, lifting the book in appreciation.

Cal nodded.

"Welp," Mike slowly stood. "The road calls. The next gig awaits." He handed the joint to me.

I tucked the book under my left arm, accepted the joint, and shook Mike's hand.

"Good luck out there."

"Yeah yeah! You too." I was still in a bit of a state of shock.

Mike nodded. Cal gave a brief salute of acknowledgement. They both disappeared into the bus which started its journey to the next town.

I smoked the last of the joint as I watched the bus drive off into the night.

***

today, everywhere i've gone by seth kaye

my failures have been served to me

on silver platters

and i've feasted on them

because of my great hunger

every face has been a mirror

catching me in the act

a real time live feed

a long receipt

showing me exactly what i've paid for

no credit will soften

the heavy clunk of my spirits

hitting the concrete

floor of my storehouses

maybe one day

i'll make transactions with these people

using their same currency

no longer offering

what i have of myself to give,   or

maybe one day

making a fair trade

will mean the exchange

of one good for another

LIKE THE SUN
by londyn rayne

---

like the sun

in the dead of night

pain knows how to veil its face

and still shed light

then rise again after it parades

as moonlight

like the sun

pain replays

casting harmful rays

without the burn, we're not alive

but we,

like the sun

surrounded by heavy clouds of mercy

revive

to soak the sky with dawn

BINGE SINNER
BY TANNER JOHNS

the binge sinner
bulimic
and purging in daylight—
the speed of which
still slower
than how quickly
you pulled the words out of him;

had to say it in the dark.

away from the Bruce Waynes
or whoever else gets it right
before he does

clears his throat
spits in a sink that won't drain;
it makes him angry
how the sins clog like hair.
a dirty Caravaggio
watches the phlegm float around
like Rorschach blots
and paints fingers
down his throat.

and looks up;
a black smile
chokes out the words,
pushing and shoving
between fat feelings
and sloth:

and finds he has no tongue.

THE MAGICAL MINIATURE GOLF COURSE OF POBLANO BEACH

BY CLAY WATERS

This was the spot

Right?

Alyssa pulled the rental car off the road, stepped into the drainage ditch, and stared at the place where the sign for *Poblano Beach Miniature Golf* had once stood.

Or had it been more beside the lamp? There was no one left to ask.

Alyssa was surprised to spot no beer cans or used condoms, only the benign ravagement of time: four shriveled palms and a couple of wooden mascots still standing. Too ugly to swipe, too dull to destroy, the rest had splintered where they'd stood, even the gigantic T-Rex (not as gigantic as she'd remembered). That left only the eighteen shallow sunken pools of artificial grass that had once comprised *Poblano Beach Miniature Golf.*

Alyssa waited. But no tears came. Emptied of emotion, in Dr. Taylor's phrase. Here it stood: the place where nothing had happened. The course she had expended endless miserable hours on at her father's insistence, trying to entice people off the road and onto the course. Other children would stare at her, the 11-year-old knocking a pink ball around alone like an orphan. She'd imagine she was a little mini-golf pro, but no one had been impressed.

Inevitably, Father would come out from under the account books and do the cheery Disney thing. But he lacked the touch, and quickly became overbearing, giving unwanted tips to sprites already squirming at the prospect of missing Mickey for some slightly dumpy miniature golf.

Miniature Golf. Not Mini Golf, certainly not Goofy Golf. No Goof in her father's soul, and maybe the visitors picked up on it. His free-floating anxiety had rubbed off on his twitchy daughter. It had done her short game no good.

Dr. Taylor had signed off on the jaunt, with reservations. "Just need to slay some demons. That's a metaphor, by the way," she had clarified, smiling nice and wide for his benefit. She had packed pills but hadn't cracked the bottle so far. The doctor had also given her a verbal assignment, one she was dawdling over.

As always, the voice in her head replied. Gently sarcastic, but mostly on her side. She hadn't told Dr. Taylor about the voice yet. He was an elderly gent, and she didn't want to give him more than he could handle at once.

She stopped on the 14th hole. The home of Lucky the Leprechaun, still standing, though a bit worse for wear.

Get it over with, she thought, imagining how she stood out, a reedy redhead, perched like a crane in the middle of an abandoned mini-golf, and delivered her sentence: "I forgive you, father."

There was a flare-up and puff of smoke. Whirling to see if she'd trodden upon a firework popper, she instead encountered a rosy-cheeked little man squatting stiffly over the 14th Hole. "Who is that disturbing my rest!?" It bellowed.

This is what you get for going off the pills, Alyssa pondered from a place slightly at an angle to herself, looking at the curiosity in a cutaway green suit and wide-brimmed country hat moving stiffly and leaning (of course) on a shillelagh, releasing wooden shavings with each stiff, squeaking turn of his neck.

Strange laughter streamed unbidden from her mouth. All her life she'd worried about going crazy, like her mother. She didn't have to worry any more.

Well. She would play along. "You're Lucky the Leprechaun," she said, aloud — as far as she could tell.

"And if it isn't sweet Alyssa, all grown-up." Lucky had acquired three dimensions: still wooden, but now thick as well as wide. Not to mention moving about and speaking in a ridiculous Irish accent.

"And what are you up to now, Alyssa? You must be two centuries old by now."

"I'm 29, actually. I live in Indiana now. Yonder way, I guess," she pointed. Her father had ended up dying outside Indianapolis, for reasons too pathetic to ponder. Drink had been the accepted cause, but Alyssa knew the real killer. She was looking over the scene of the crime right then.

Then a happier thought came upon her. "If I catch you, you have to give me three wishes! Those are the rules!" She grabbed at Lucky; he ducked, she tried again.

"Leave me be! Leave me be, confound you!" Lucky wasn't as stiff as he looked, and nimbly dodged Alyssa's clutchings. Finally she lunged too fiercely, fell over and stayed, her giddy laughter gradually devolving into quiet sobs. The meltdown had arrived; she leaned into it like a softened-up old pillow, perversely comfortable, her cheek resting against the artificial grass. It was threadbare but still pleasantly abrasive as she calmly sobbed.

A pair of oft-mended green shoes crept into her blurred vision. "Stop that, now," Lucky said, softer. "See, you're messing up my shoes, and I just mended them."

That's when Alyssa realized everything happening was actually happening.

So the spot had been cursed after all. She felt awe, relief, catharsis, anger. Mainly regret.

"Well. This changes things. May I ask you a question?" She monitored the airy, slightly unhinged quality of her timbre. "I'm not angry, I just need to know. Did you steal our balls?"

"Pardon?"

"All our pink balls disappeared one night."

"Pardon? Are you accusing me of stealing your precious golf balls?" Lucky's own face went pink. "Certainly! Ate them with my tea, I did! Oh yes, I brought down this mighty enterprise with my own wee hands." He flashed his yellowed fingernails, wagged one in her face. "Look here, missy, I did nothing to this place, good or ill. It was all ye father's doing. He put in the sweat but he wasn't cut out for the work. No gift of gab, no blithe spirit. He wrecked the place fine all by his wee self."

"Well who took them, then?"

"A bunch of kids one night. Your boyfriend, for one."

"Boyfriend?" Oh yeah. The parched kiss behind the waterwheel on the 5th Hole. "You mean Ben?"

"Aye, sold them to the course across the way. Wanted to get more girls to play, who knows?" He shrugged stiffly.

"So you didn't put an old Irish hex on the place." Alyssa felt peculiarly disappointed. "But there is magic here?"

"Aye. But only a few could see us stirring about, mostly wee ones.

Others just saw the flat cutouts. You could see us before, in spots, when you were wearied at night from your play."

Play? Ha. "I thought I was just tired."

"What changed, I wonder."

"Selective serotonin reuptake inhibitors."

"Pardon?"

"Drugs."

Lucky nodded. "Change the brain, they do. Anyway, there's only two of us left now. But all we mascots had full personalities, once. Something to do with vestigial energy. That's what Danny the Dolphin said, before he faded away. He was the smart one."

Alyssa remembered the happy dolphin on the 6th hole. "So are all things alive? Like golf balls? Like stuffed animals? Do they miss us when we abandon them like this?" She gestured about.

"Oh, don't start crying again, it's not as bad as all that. We don't have the angst you poor sods do. Like your father: Thick with worry." Lucky pointed to a spot over her head. "You've got it too. Like a gray rainbow." A pause. "I know of your Father," he said gravely. "What of your mum?"

"I never had a mother."

Lucky set his tongue to retort, then seemed to think better.

"It's very clean here," she said, to clear the air. One could still play the course. Theoretically.

"It better be. This is my home. The lusty lads and lassies come to park, or bring their dog to leave shite, but I frighten them off, make no mistake."

"How?"

"They may not hear me, but they sure know when I throw a stone out of the dark."

Sigh. She would have to tell the resident of the 14th Hole the real reason she had returned. Later. "So what else can you do?"

"I can mend shoes and find gold."

"Really?"

"No. That's a load of ole' crap! Excepting the shoes, that's true enough." He flashed his gold buckles. "Two centuries I've had these."

"Two centuries? Ah, go shave your beard, Lucky."

The leprechaun harrumphed. "By the by, that is not the name I would have chosen. If it were up to me, I'd be called Cairbre, or Searlas."

"Something sensible."

"Aye. Hmm..." A suspicious squint. "You have developed an odd sense of humor in your old age, Alyssa. So, what has brought you back after so many years?"

"School reunion." That was half the truth, anyway. "I stayed 10 minutes grinning like a goon and no one even said hello."

Lucky gestured toward the 13th hole. "Argh. Look what the cat hath drug in."

Alyssa found it hard to speak. "Oh goodness. It's Red Bird." A pause. "Can I go see him?"

"If you wish. Mind you, he's a bit surly when he's just woken. And just about any other time, for that."

She turned and made what must have looked a very silly bow. "You're the Red Bird," she said, feeling her face redden as well.

> **❝ From there she putted calmly through the course, hands steady, relying wholly on muscle memory, the outline of each stroke appearing like a schematic in her head.**

"Well of course I am!" The Red Bird huffed, twangy, surprisingly Texan. "See my wings?" He flapped them fearsomely, but even at full wingspan he was just two feet wide and two feet tall, so it registered as wasted effort.

Perhaps the artist had enjoyed his work that day, for there was a life and energy to Red Bird than the others— especially poor, shapeless Sammy the Shark— had lacked. Still, the bird had more feathers than necessary and didn't look particularly aerodynamic -- more like an aggrieved, undersized ostrich. Had the eyes always been so fierce? Not at all like the—

"Oh goodness."

"Pardon?"

She whispered, "I just realized. The Red Bird. He was based on the Orange Bird all along! From Disney? I never noticed it then because I wasn't allowed to watch." Disney was the competition with the mini-golf, though it was possible no one had told Disney that.

"Never saw a Disney? Well I'll be banjaxed. Would love to visit."

"You'd best bring all ye gold then. Banjaxed?"

A stiff shrug. "Sometimes things just spill off my tongue. Besides, I'm stuck in the shire, see?" He kicked out; she heard a tiny thud against an invisible barrier.

"Whoa. Anyway, Red Bird reminds me of The Orange Bird."

"Gosh, I wouldn't tell him that."

"What was that?" Came Red Bird's caw from behind. Lucky winced. Red Bird stalked up to the edge of his patch of green. "I am being talked about."

Alyssa gulped in the face of the strutting ball of feathers and anger. "I was just saying that you look like a Disney character. Another bird."

"Nonsense. There is no other bird like me."

"I'll show you," she said, sensing it was a mistake but also getting kind of angry at the preening little shit-bird. She retrieved the coffee mug from her car and walked it over. "See?" She pointed. "That's the Orange Bird."

The Red Bird tilted his outsized head as far as it could go. "Ha! I knew you were lying. That's a lousy copy of me."

"Actually, the Orange Bird was around before you were even a drop of paint."

"That's another lie."

"And do you know the other great thing about the Orange Bird? He didn't talk."

"Hmmph." With that the Red Bird turned, waddled to his hole and stuck his beak in it.

"You've hurt his feelings now," Lucky said reproachfully. "It's better he sleep, frankly. I try to be kind, but he makes it diff--see, there he goes." The big beak had stopped bobbing, and the eyes had lost their fire.

They waited for the transformation to complete, for the bird to shrink into damaged wood again.

Alyssa swiped away a tear. "Red Bird was my favorite. Is he the only other one left?"

"Aye. And he's on the way out. This patch is strong with magic, but you still need a forceful personality to survive."

"You must have eternal life, then."

"Hush now." But a grin enlivened Lucky's face.

She kneaded her forehead. "I should go to bed as well."

"Surely you're not leaving without at least shooting a round?"

"I will never pick up a club again."

"Enough with that babble." And then she had a club in her hand, though she didn't remember picking one up.

"I'm going to need a ball. A pink one," she challenged. "And some crappy '80s music."

"I can top that." Lucky fished a shiny penny-whistle from his prodigious pockets and began piping an ethereal tune. Somehow she had alighted upon the 1st Hole, once home to sad-eyed Ollie the Octopus. A pink ball lay on the pad beneath her. She lined up to accommodate her left-handed stroke. She swung, then ambled over to find the ball already in the hole.

Well, #1 was a gimme.

She visualized the second hole and hit without looking up.

Perfect.

From there she putted calmly through the course, hands steady, relying wholly on muscle memory, the outline of each stroke appearing like a schematic in her head.

She finished the back nine with only the flickering street lamp for light. Not even the stiffened form of Red Bird threw her off her game.

When the last ball rattled in on 18 and disappeared, she heard Lucky clicking his heels. "A twenty-five! My goodness. Must have been the music, eh?"

Alyssa tilted her head, as if still listening for the tune. "That beats the course record by two strokes." She laid the club and ball down and sat cross-legged beside her new friend. "There was one other reason I came down, Lucky."

"A ha. The penny is dropping."

"I came down to sell this property."

"I thought you were telling less than you knew." Lucky folded his arms and went into a sulk before becoming suddenly alive again. "Well, you have a say, don't you?"

"Yeah, they can't do anything unless I give the official word. We could keep it as is."

"You can do better than that. Open the place back up. The groundwork is still here. You just played a round yourself."

"You don't really mean..." But in a flash she saw it all.

She gazed down upon Lucky's fat contented face and exhaled, at last. Squatters rights for old wooden mascots. She really was insane. "Alright, you plucky little bastard, I'll do it."

*

Alyssa moved back to Florida, refurbished and reopened the property as *Poblano Beach Magical Miniature Golf Course.* She put in a soft-ice cream and recreated the old look (which had circled back into style anyway), embellished with some garish mascots, put together by a local art student. Whatever magic left unmined, failed to rub off on the new arrivals, but Lucky was more vigorous than ever.

And every couple of weeks, often in the ambivalent hour before sunset...leprechaun sightings.

Much snapping of pics ensued, with intriguing, leprechaun-shaped blotches resistant to the smarty-pants collective of Internet experts. Playing by ear, Alyssa let the phenomenon grow naturally online, forward to forward, share to share. The local weekly ran an article: "The Magic Hole of Poblano Beach?" A web outfit came and did a ghost-hunting special with infrared cameras and all the accompanying silliness, which was great for business, though Lucky got a little steamed when she read him a review off her tablet. "They don't believe I exist, do they?"

"Perhaps it's for the best," she said, counting the take at evening's close via flashlight at the 14th hole. "Did anyone see you today?"

Lucky shook his head. "Just a wee one, and an addled gent with hair long as a girl, and dirty as a rat's nest. Had this put-on Irish accent and wouldn't stop jabbering about the craic and Jameson. Blech!"

"How do you know what Jameson tastes like?"

"It's blended whiskey, isn't it? Blech!"

Red Bird departed over the summer. He and Alyssa had reconciled somewhat by the end, mostly by not conversing too much. She got off the pills.

Her birthday approached, and with it a suspicious uplift in Lucky's demeanor. "It shall be your birthday soon, Alyssa. 'The Dirty Thirty,' I believe it is called."

"And how did you know?"

"You've only talked about it all month. Mostly to that boy who's always hanging about. Alan, his name?"

"Yes. And please never say 'Dirty Thirty' again."

"So, what is your heart's desire?"

Alyssa put her finger to her chin, pretending to ponder. "Maybe... nah, that would be hokey."

"What is it, then?" Lucky asked with a sigh.

"Never mind. I have something for you instead." Then she bent and whispered into Lucky's ear the name she had found, a long name, a name with hills and valleys, with rills and grooves.

The leprechaun said nothing, in fact went a bit quiet the rest of the day.

*

Alyssa rose in the morning, drove to work — worrying a bit over whether she had wounded her friend's tangled feelings — and stood staring, mouth agape, at what was hanging over the clubhouse roof.

The rainbow poured right into the cup at the 14th hole. Lucky waited there, looking quite pleased with himself, in a patch of indigo. "I fear there's no pot of gold," he said.

Alyssa did not abuse her height by picking up Lucky, but she had nothing against patting the top of his hat. "You're my pot of gold."

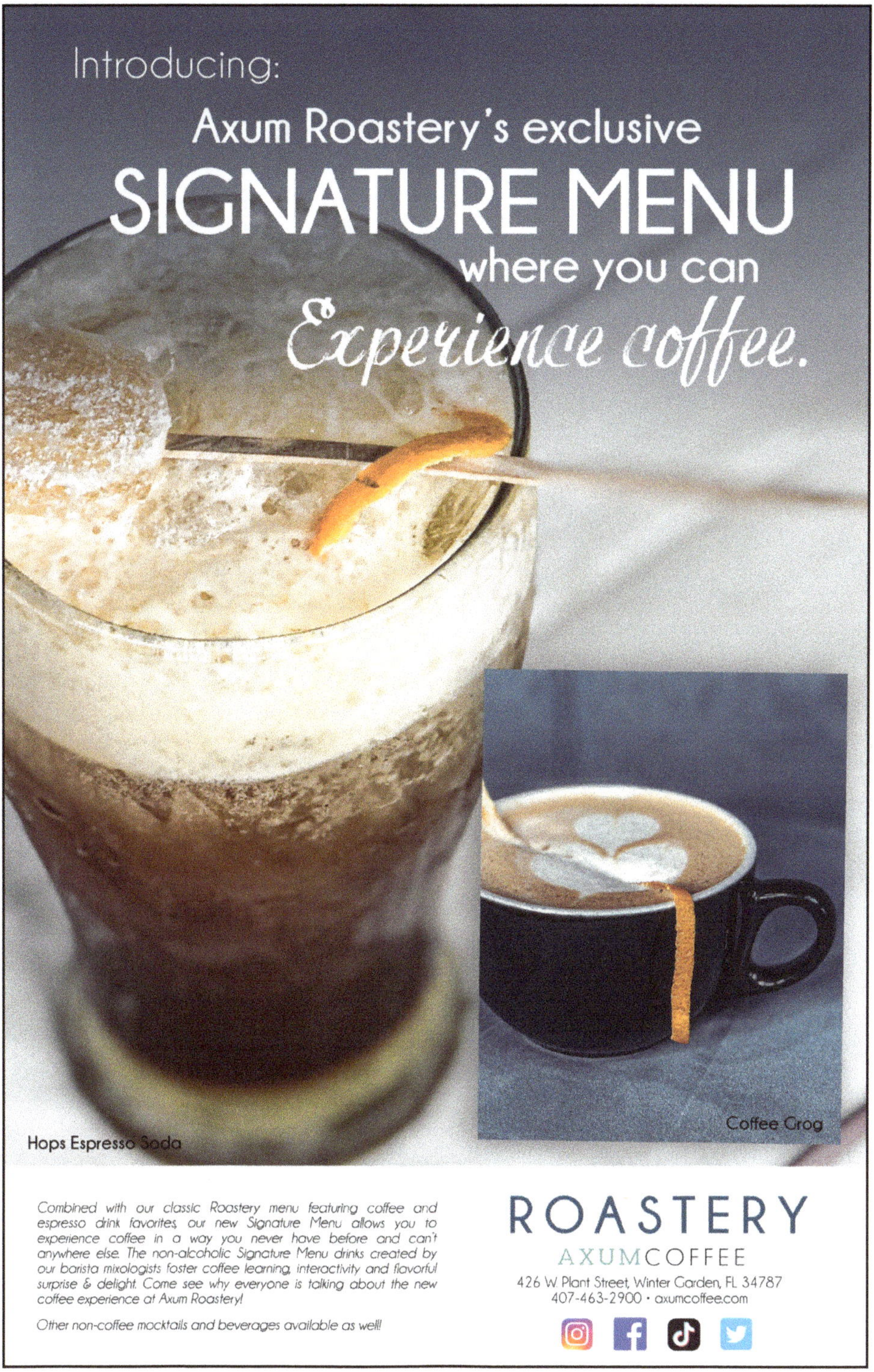
Introducing:
Axum Roastery's exclusive
SIGNATURE MENU
where you can
Experience coffee.
Hops Espresso Soda
Coffee Grog
Combined with our classic Roastery menu featuring coffee and espresso drink favorites, our new Signature Menu allows you to experience coffee in a way you never have before and can't anywhere else. The non-alcoholic Signature Menu drinks created by our barista mixologists foster coffee learning, interactivity and flavorful surprise & delight. Come see why everyone is talking about the new coffee experience at Axum Roastery!
Other non-coffee mocktails and beverages available as well!
ROASTERY
AXUMCOFFEE
426 W. Plant Street, Winter Garden, FL 34787
407-463-2900 • axumcoffee.com

AUTHOR FOCUS
WITH BLAKE SLAUGHTER

Blake Slaughter has been writing since the age of eight when he first began scribbling song lyrics. By twleve, he was crafting stories and since then has added poetry to his resume. A freethinker, Blake walks his own path, both in writing and in life. Currently, he is working on two poetry collections and when he has down time likes to catch up on movies and spend time with friends. This is the fourth issue of Storyteller to feature his work. We caught up with Blake recently to ask about what he's been up to and also gain some insight into his thoughts on writing in general.

In this new world of quarantining and social distancing, many creatives are feeling a pressure to spend any newly found free time in pursuit of creative endeavors. Is this a pressure you're feeling as well? If so, how are you managing it?

I do feel as though I have an obligation to use my creativity with this spare time given to me, but regularly find myself uninspired or lacking the will. However, I have begun writing a book of poetry, which I am really ecstatic about because I think it's unlike anything I've written before; more personal. Rupi Kaur's work has had a lot to do with my determination to write lately.

The global pandemic we are currently facing, along with a lot of pain and suffering, also seems to have brought a host of lessons to be learned. What is one revelation you hope society takes away from our current situation? What is a personal revelation you have experienced during this situation?

I was already a big "earth advocate," but seeing a major decline in pollution during this pandemic has opened my eyes even further to environmental issues and climate change. Seeing clearer water and skies is something that everyone should not only be overjoyed by, but endeavor to preserve. I've also learned to take nothing for granted; a brief visit with friends, traveling, or a trip to the movies to see a highly-anticipated film.

Your stories always have a strong sense of place. What real world settings and environments inspire you the most?

Thank you! I think I can obtain inspiration from anywhere; whether that be from the unique shape of a building, the way two people interact with each other, or something on the local news. The world can be a pretty scary and dramatic place, so I don't always have to travel too far to spark creation. I do, however, get a lot of my inspiration from visual art which in turn leads me to imagine that as I create my plot and characters.

Do you have any literary pet peeves?

I'm not a big fan of stories that have rushed dialogue or don't bother to describe much of the protagonist's situation; especially when told from the viewpoint of a teenager or young adult. It can sometimes generate the impression that young people are lazy and unappreciative of their surroundings.

There's a lot of conversation surrounding the topic of writer's block, but have you ever experienced reader's block? If so, how do you respond to it? Is there a book you are able to turn to time and time again, no matter how stuck you are feeling?

I often find myself turning to poetry if I feel lost because sometimes my brain is unwilling to process anything too drawn-out. A book like The Sun and Her Flowers is an exceptional work

of art whose passages I could read endlessly, as I sometimes find they verbalize some of my own experiences, which can truly bring comfort in times of unease.

Is there a book or author you once hated, but have grown to appreciate?

Though this may be incredibly difficult for the people who know me to believe, I wasn't exactly head over heels for Stephen King's work when I first picked up Pet Sematary at about 12 years old, but I've come to appreciate his stories of the world's darker side that not everyone sees. Pet Sematary has also become one of my favorite novels as well.

Do your characters ever "stick" with you, even after you've finished their stories?

Absolutely! Even if I were to write sequels to the stories, I would continue to wonder what other predicaments may arise in that character's life long after the final chapter concludes.

Check out Blake's latest collection of poems, titled "The Difference Between Shadows and Silhouettes", in the pages that follow.

THE DIFFERENCE BETWEEN SHADOWS AND SILHOUETTES:

A COLLECTION OF POEMS

by Blake Slaughter

Flower Crowns

Paths of splendor reside in southern hills
amidst persecution from neighbors. Come one. Only one.
Break from purported uprightness only for a minute—
the grass awaits. Its dew is reborn with the morn
though it brings it no life.

Although these thorns the roses bared for us
go unnoticed, they are unlike that of those that prick
the skin. They are straight forward, clean cut—
a picture of perfection surrounded by holy light.
They never prick the skin. They are the epicenter
of normal behavior.

The influence from such elements withdrew me
from my miserable anonymity, forcing me
to recognize that I was experiencing
an Indian summer. An absence of unrequited love
unbeknownst to the insular system was met with
innocent passion.

The pine needles— all the needles
brushed against me and brought only contentment
in place of supposed agony. To the right
my light, my glorious burning star
flares in unison with me
as the neighbors wallow away in their prejudice
and illiberal tendencies.

Wayfarer

Solitary confinement. Voluntary, but dreadful
nonetheless. The echoes of the green and yellow forest
are far, but not untouchable. They watch me
in my home and taunt me with their threatening
weapons of psychology. Domineering voices, you bastards
you will never take me. Whenever I leave
from hiding, they pursue me indefatigably,
but they will always be at a distance.

The Elder harms me and wishes the fires
of hell to consume me, but she knows not what she does.
She is a child plagued with white hair. The Red Man
struck me only once, but the words that followed
will rebound off the walls of my remote entrapment
for the remainder of my lifetime. I am slow
to understand my setting because I drift
amid the clouds, but have never stood closer to hell.

Don the mask.
Beloved dominator of emotion
the one I seek out in disheartened periods. Habitually
these worries plague me without cure, only shade.
Prevent my uncountable riddles, unbeknownst to the masses
from seeing the luminous glow and preserve the confidences
held for others. Keep me holding on.

Am I An Illusion?
When you teach sons and daughters
that hatred is affection, they grow to fall in love
with loathing themselves. Your drunkenness
and ignorance will end in punishments
harsher than hangover and rebuttal.
Regret is a silent killer. Silence is louder
than any words we could shout.

I dream of walking free among marigolds,
but I'm confined to this small and featureless room.
Am I an illusion yet? Am I a celluloid film
burned into a stubborn brain refusing to let me go?
After all, why would I remain in such a restrained space
governed by hands that forbid me to grow? You
doubt my worth. I doubt your sanity.

I am a wild animal caged amidst palms
and paradise. I am the act of lust in the land
of abstinence. I am the defiant son of a world who
desires my compliance, the son of parents who once
shared my dreams before they had to find ones of
their own. Surely, I am an illusion in a world of conjurers
too engaged in their enchantments
to bring me back.

Blood Stained Sand

What led you to me? I dare to ask it, if I may,
of others too. Was it doubt in that of which is true: the
forceful upheaval of the uneven road ahead to
behind? Was it parents poisoning virgin minds?

Where we once found butterflies in speedbumps
and shopping cart rides, we now seek vulgarity
and convincing lies. There is a Heaven and Hell
a good and bad, and many years in one to be
had. One might say bliss is a bird that takes flight
before it can be captured— one that leaves you
to perish in a private rapture.

I could tell you that what you may find is paradise
in the midst of panic attacks, as breaking hearts is
an art I've always excelled at. However, I cannot
tell lies without a voice— I am a truthful being
without choice. Walk with me awhile, in happiness
and pain. I'll show you who will leave and who will remain.
Though this may be a process you'll come to detest
you have my word: it's for the best.

*

PINBALLS

BY LARRY GRIFFFIN

Seth Driver's mother had been drunk

most afternoons of his childhood. She would scream at him if he hadn't taken out the trash and done the dishes by the time she woke up, groggy and lopsided, at 7 p.m.

She kept an ashtray, filled to the brim, and the house tended to smell like unwashed laundry. It wasn't that she had no heart; it was just that she couldn't control her worst impulses. She'd have moments of caring, but also plenty more of dereliction. Like when she left him at the laundromat while she got drunk for two hours, and then he'd have to ride home with her and her boy-toys, who had nudie magazines and grease-stained toolkits in the back of their trucks. They'd call him 'Sport,' with a leering condescension he wasn't able to name when he was young.

And now he was 30 and standing in their old trailer, going through her personal effects. They'd said it was a heart attack. She was 52. It seemed a waste to Seth.

He sifted through two beat-up cardboard boxes full of old tax envelopes, receipts with notes drunkenly scrawled on them, and pictures of the two of them; her leggy, ash-blonde-haired self, clad in faded denim and him, a scrawny kid with his father's dark, curly hair, clad in clothes too big, purloined from the local Goodwill. In the pictures, they leaned against her junker of a station wagon, which, over the years, had taken on the pure color of rust, tag-teamed by sun and time. In one picture, she had her arms around him, protective mother-bear, in a sunny park. It didn't even tell a tenth of the story.

There wasn't much he needed here. He'd take two or three pictures for posterity. Robin, who worked at his favorite bar in Chicago, had lent an ear to him and, when he said he was going to clean his mother's trailer out, said oh, keep some things, for your kids.

But Seth wasn't going to have kids. He remembered his own childhood as something rangy and awkward; constant growing pains, nothing he'd want to inflict on another. So that was that. He stood in his mother's old trailer, with its worn beige carpet, the wooden wall with the patched-up white hole where he'd thrown a baseball one time, the kitchen where his mother had often filled the trash can with empty beer bottles and cans. This was the end of the line. A coda.

#

He went to a bar called Shanahan's, which was, incidentally, the same place his mother would go when she left him at the laundromat. There were better places in Crescent City now, all the craft cocktail joints down by city hall with their Christmas lights and board games. But Shanahan's was the place you went when you weren't in the mood for the innate posturing of those places. It had a football pennant on the wall, the TV was cracked and dim, and the bartender was a crabby old geezer, the same guy since the late '80s, old Bert McGraw with his famous walrus mustache.

Seth didn't expect anyone to recognize him here. He'd been gone for too damn long, taking photographs up north. But Bert McGraw's hard, odd eyes fixed on him. "Well, Jesus, if it ain't Mr. Big City Driver." His voice, a booming baritone, echoed through the old place– this place was so rickety it was liable to fall down in a hurricane.

"Hey, Bert." Seth sat down and rotated on the stool to get comfortable, hearing the thing creak and whine.

"You come back here to gloat in our faces some more?" Bert grinned his usual grin, which was confrontational, something edgy behind it.

"Actually, my mom died." Seth rested his elbows on the bar. He didn't have it in him to explain that he often struggled for rent in Chicago these days, scraping by on family photos and school ones now and then, as well as the good will of his landlord. He didn't have it in him to say that everything just seemed to keep getting more expensive.

Bert's face drooped, his mouth opening in a small shocked 'o' shape. "Sharon's passed? Well, shit." He turned to the bar, which was full of the usual gaggle of barflies: men with sports jerseys, and women in shirts too tight for 60 year olds. "Why don't we have a moment of silence, raise our glasses?"

And so they all did, albeit an imperfect silence, fraught with grumbles. Seth ordered a Bud Light. Bert passed it across the bar to him.

There was one woman at the bar who stood out. She was skinny and had a complexion so pale he almost thought her a ghost. Her hair, long and chocolate-brown and curly, stretched almost all the way down her back in a cascade. She wore a light tan coat and new-looking denim jeans and stylish-looking boots. She caught him looking. "You OK there, bud?"

He startled back to reality. "Oh, yeah. Yeah. Sorry." He averted his eyes and sipped his beer.

She had a martini in front of her, and sipped it from a tiny pink straw. "This thing's terrible."

He looked back at her, noticing the drink. "Oh, yeah. From what I gather, Bert introduced those just 'cause the new trendy places were coming in. He threw together like, the cheapest possible ingredients and started putting it on the menu."

The woman's face unfolded into a grin that was so damn warm it lit up her whole face, and suddenly she didn't seem oddly thin, but, instead, perfectly beautiful. "That's fucking hilarious."

"Yeah, well, small town, what are you gonna do?" Seth told himself to quit looking at her like she was an art piece in a museum. He couldn't just gawk. It wasn't high school anymore. He looked at the far wall, where he could see himself reflected in the mirrored Guinness sign. He could see the bags under his eyes and that his hair was getting a bit long.

The woman sipped more of her martini. "I don't know why I keep drinking this. I guess, well, I got the babysitter."

"You've got kids?" Seth grinned, leaning on his right elbow, looking at her with a kind of curiosity.

She glared at him. "Yeah, yeah. Make your jokes."

He shifted back to an upright sitting position. "No, I mean it. You're probably a great mom."

"'Yeah. Good save, pal." She polished off her martini, and flagged Bert down for another.

Seth took a breath and shifted his arms, folding them in front of his chest. "Hey, I didn't mean to offend you."

She was looking at him with a kind of bemused acidity, but she didn't leave her stool. "Could've fooled me."

"What's your name?" Seth extended a hand. "I'm Seth. I used to live here."

She looked at his hand, examining it. Then she shook it. "I'm Stella."

"Stella. Nice name."

"Thank you." She mock-curtsied, even though she was sitting down, and Seth felt something spark in him like a match.

"So, what brings you to town? I've never seen you before." Seth got off his stool and moved to the one closer to her. He made himself comfortable there.

She looked away for a moment, as if expecting someone to come through the door. Then she looked back at him. "I, well, you know, I had a friend here. I needed a place to get out of town."

Seth thought of Chicago, with all its avenues, all the towers stretching up so far you couldn't see. "I get what you mean."

She nodded. "Sometimes, yeah, it's just like... you just need to get away."

Seth nodded, tilting his beer bottle to his lips. "And what did you need to get away from?"

She laughed and shook her head, her hair batting around her pale skin, invading the space around her. "No, no. I'm not quite that drunk."

"Let's go out, then. Let's get properly acquainted, so you can tell me." Seth could feel the grin on his face. It'd been a while since he had been attracted to someone this way.

She looked at him with skeptical eyes. "Are you just trying to scam me here?"

He raised his hands in surrender. "Hey, no. No way."

She shook her head and grinned. "Trick question. Y'all are always trying to scam somebody. What's a date, anyway? What's a date but a scam?"

He just looked at her. She laughed. Then she wrote her number on a napkin and passed it over to him.

\#

They met at Bottle Rockets Lounge, an expansive reformed warehouse with hard concrete floors and wood picnic tables set up around the main area. The bar was long, and stocked with all manner of beer and wine, and even harder liquor. The bartender, Elissa, liked to show movies at night, cult classics, old '70s horror films no one had heard of. It was a raucous, but somehow artful, place. There were old pinball machines in one corner, a Super Nintendo set up in another. The walls were adorned with strange abstract paintings from local artists.

Elissa, with her dyed green hair and nose piercing, greeted Seth and Stella as they walked in. She was chewing bubble gum. Seth ordered a beer for himself, a hazy IPA, and Stella asked for white wine. They sat across from each other at a table. She smiled at him. "This is a nice place. Much nicer than that bar from yesterday."

"Just never say that in Shanahan's." Seth sipped his drink.

"Why? What's the worst they can do?" Her grin was mischievous, and even her eyes seemed to be laughing.

Seth shrugged. "It ain't out of the realm of possibility. They keep to themselves down here. Make their own rules."

"Ooh. Well, in that case, my lips are sealed."

"I hope not for too long." He sipped his beer. She laughed.

"You're pretty funny, you know?"

Then she was looking at the pinball machine. She asked if he wanted to play.

\#

Setting their drinks on a table by the machine, Seth watched as Stella geared up to play. The machine was Back to the Future themed, and had all the trappings: a DeLorean in the middle, a futuristic type world with dark blue shades and tall buildings, a Western setting with yellow hues and little paper cacti, all of it a maze where you had to try and navigate the little ball, or else certain death would be imminent.

He watched her shoulders move, her face a mask of concentration as she pulled the little levers. The ball rocketed around the map. Her eyes widened and her mouth formed a little 'O' as the ball looked like it was about to fall into one of the holes that'd mean she won. "This game's so damn hard. But I like it. Keeps you on your toes, right?"

Seth observed her trial by fire. The ball went every which way and hit the wall, almost falling. Then she'd flip a lever and the ball would be airborne again, zipping around like it was on crack. "You're fucking good."

She glanced at him for a brief second, hair in her face, mouth a wild energetic grin. "I practice whenever I can. I guess I'm competitive."

Then the ball fell in the winning hole, and she cheered, pumping both fists into the air. He clapped her on the shoulder. She turned around and wrapped her arms around him, a tight embrace, not just one of those friendly polite ones. He could smell her lavender perfume, and her hair was soft against his cheek. When she separated from him, there was a blush on her cheek. "Do you want to try?"

He looked at the pinball machine. Then back at her. "Let's finish these drinks and take a walk, huh?"

\#

They walked around Lake Ashley, a spacious three-mile circle that joggers could be found traversing most mornings, coated in sweat, blaring music from earbuds. Now it was just them. The air was chilly and Stella wrapped her coat around herself. Seth noticed and sidled just a bit closer as they walked. "Want me to warm you up?"

She made a face at him, amused, but eyeing him skeptically. "There it is. I knew it... the grift."

He raised his hands in surrender, stepping a bit away from her as he grinned. "Hey, I was just offering. Cold is a bad thing to be."

"Okay, okay." She stepped a little closer to him again.

They passed a raccoon scuttling away from a dumpster. There were yellow warm lights in the houses. Stella looked at the lights and then at Seth. "It's fun to walk at night, because you never know who you'll end up seeing through the windows, you know? It could be anyone."

Seth nudged her with his elbow. "Didn't know you were a peeping Tom."

She let out a high giggle. "No, no! It's just interesting to see peoples' lives. And plus, we only just met, you don't know anything about me yet."

"That's true. I'll concede that."

They walked a little more, coming to a thicket of trees, shadows inside, a winding labyrinth. Stella looked at the lake and then at the sky. "It's so nice to be out, you know? I spend so much time with the kids. I take 'em out as much as I can, but… just the looks I get when I do that, it becomes so exhausting…"

"The looks?"

"Just the people judging me, like they're waiting for one of the kids to have a tantrum. Like, they assume I've not tried to teach them how to act. It's like, they're nine and seven, not fucking two year olds." She'd folded her arms and was looking down, looking smaller somehow.

"Man, fuck that, then."

"I know." She was looking at him with such an intensity. Like a meteor, Seth thought incoherently. "You're really nice, though. A lot of guys seriously never want to go out once they find out I've got kids. I never understand why that is."

Seth had his hands in his pockets. "They think it's like, some weird violation, like it'd be stepping on something else that's already going. They think they'd rather have someone who's, ah, a blank slate, or whatever. I don't know. That's what my friends seem to think, back up north."

"You got some real piece of shit friends, then." She was smiling to herself in a way that suggested this wasn't a shared moment. Her arms, folded tight around her midriff, seemed like a barrier to the outside. "I mean, sorry. But yeah. I dunno, though. I think guys just don't want to be fathers. It's amazing that families ever get started. I feel like, for some women, it's blackmail… like they make the guys do it."

"Do you wish you'd done that?"

"Wow, well, that's an interesting question." She flipped her hair over her shoulder. "I dunno. I mean, I really don't think we were better off, well, before."

He could sense he had wandered into uncomfortable territory. He always did this. It felt like he had no filter between his brain's darkest recesses and the things you'd say on a date. The things that came into his mind were often so damn strange.

They reached the full circle of the lake. They were back facing the town with its little lights in the distance and dark hollow stores closed for the night. Stella shifted and faced him, arms folded, her face somber and stoic. "I guess I just ought to tell you – I was a member of this Mormon convent up in Utah for, like, years. That's where I had my kids and where my husband still is. Well, ex-husband. Or… well, I don't really know, I guess."

He heard the weight behind the words. He pictured bearded men in robes, angrily plotting, wagging their fingers, a dusty village with horses and carts and one-story buildings heated by fire.

"And, uh, well, the truth is that we left the place and are trying to find a way to live on our own." She had lost all her humor from before. She was dead-serious.

"Shit. That sounds, uh, really fucked up. Is everything OK?"

They'd begun walking back up the small slope to the parking area near the bar. She stopped and wrung her hands, as if she didn't know what to do, and when she spoke, her voice was high and nervous. "It was this ultra-conservative, prehistoric kind of place. My parents were like that – I mean, they started out just normal, just a bit afraid of the world, and then they were suddenly dragging me out of school and to this rural convent out in the deep country, and they just lived there. They wanted that. It was all farmwork and weird school classes about old puritan values and stuff, all done in rooms without air conditioning. For fun we either read old books or went and played by the river, if our parents would let us.

"And I guess I was sort of brainwashed into the whole deal. I got married to this guy and we had kids, and then I was in my 20s and decided I needed to go, 'cause, you know, I was seeing my kids start to understand the world. There was this moment of clarity where I could see that I didn't want the same thing for them."

They arrived at her car, a white Acura. She looked at him and watched him understand all of it. He licked his lips, adjusted his hair with the palm of his hand. He said, "I mean, wow. That was not what I expected you to say at all."

She had an anxious look now, self-conscious, her brows high, her mouth a tight line. "I just... I felt like I ought to be straight. You know... if we see each other again."

"So you want to see me again?" He felt a grin coming on, even a bit of a blush. He put his hands in his pockets.

"Of course that's your takeaway." She looked assured. The doubt seemed to seep away. She punched him in the shoulder, friendly-like.

\#

Seth decided to stay for a few days more. He didn't have a plan anymore. His mother was gone, and the funeral was done. He lazed about in the old trailer, smoking weed on the couch and watching old reruns of Battlestar Galactica and Buffy the Vampire Slayer on a Roku he'd purchased. His place in Chicago held no particular sway, and his lease was almost up anyway. Maybe it would be time to go again soon.

He texted his friend Trent, who had moved back to the area a few years after high school. Trent told him to come by.

Trent lived in an upper-story apartment near downtown, the gentrified area, with his girlfriend Bethany. It was a cluttered place, but it all felt methodical somehow; like they'd put it there for a movie set, all the home-spun signs, the paintings, the souvenirs from beach shops. Bethany, red-headed and smiling wide, greeted him at the door. He could smell the smoke from the grill.

Trent was on the porch cooking a few steaks. Trent, broad-shouldered and curly-headed, greeted him with a bro-hug, stiff, clapping him on the back. The steak smelled rich and divine. "Jesus," Trent said. "It's been an age, man."

"Yeah, I guess it has." Seth remembered the two of them smoking pot under the awning of the band building as dusk fell. Trent had played the trombone, and Seth had played the clarinet. They didn't remember why they'd joined band anymore.

\#

Trent set out the steaks on plates in the dining room. Bethany had cooked steamed carrots and broccoli, which she carefully piled onto all of their plates. There was wine on the table— a deluxe-looking white. The light was warm from an elaborate-looking overhead lamp, almost as stylized as a chandelier.

"You were just in time," she said. "We were just starting to cook."

Seth drank some of the wine they'd poured. "Yeah, I didn't even know if I'd be intruding. Thanks for all this."

"Any time, man." Trent cut into the steak, silverware scraping the hard plate. He plucked a red juicy chunk into his mouth.

Bethany set her napkin in her lap as she sat down. "So, what've you been up to?"

"Oh, a little of this, a little of that. I've been taking pictures up in Chicago. I have a few friends there and I thought it'd be nice to get lost in the city a bit. But I might move on soon." He ate a carrot. Then began cutting into the steak.

Trent rested an elbow on the table, his wide-shouldered form seeming cramped here. "Really? Man, you're a fucking adventurer, huh?"

Bethany put her fork down after swallowing a piece of steak. "Yeah, we're always just envious. Just so jealous, seeing the stuff you post on social media, where you're going and all of that."

#

As a young man, Seth never felt like he'd belonged. His mother, in her late 30s then, had glared at him as he was done with high school. He was standing in the living room and she'd said when I was your age, my parents just kicked me out.

And he'd said, Oh.

And she'd said, Do you have any plans for your future?

He had been 18 and dumb, dreaming of finding bags of money and moving to Vegas to gamble, meeting a hooker with a heart of gold. Instead, he applied for a bunch of grants and scholarships and was off.

College had passed in a haze of booze and half-read textbooks. In April, after a graduation ceremony, he stood on emerald-green lawns and looked at the buildings where he'd studied until he fell asleep in the morning. It felt like he'd been booted again, as surely as his exodus from his mother's trailer. The void formed over the coming years and he got comfortable with it.

#

They were sitting on the hood of his car with paper trays of gourmet hot dogs, lavished with relish and peppers. She'd eaten a quarter of hers. There was a bit of relish on her cheek. He reached over and wiped it off.

"That's what we're doing now?" She smirked.

He wiped the relish off with his other hand. "Hey, can't have you looking like a slob."

"It's a post-feminist world. Looking like a slob is OK now, didn't anybody tell you?"

They ate their hot dogs. He felt like a high schooler again. But this was Crescent City. There wasn't anything to do, really.

Stella said, "So, I guess you're cool with all the stuff I said before, then?"

"The, ah, convent stuff, the Mormons and all? Or was it the other thing?"

She shook her head and swatted him with one hand.

He chuckled. "Hey, you gotta give me credit there."

She said, "It's just, this is really important to me." She looked away immediately. Her hands were clasped between her legs. The hotdog sat on the car hood, getting cold.

Seth put his own hotdog down. "I'm sorry."

She looked at him with a hardness to her now steely eyes and a rigid, standoffish posture. He could see a woman who'd left her whole life and traveled across the country. "It's OK, I guess. But, yeah... like, I have all this stuff in my mind. Like I was wondering if you were OK with the Mormon thing, and then my brain jumped from that to, what is it that you want out of this whole thing?"

He put his hand on hers— a reflex. He didn't even know where it came from. "Hey, I'm cool with it. Let's just, you know, keep going. I like it. I like this. I only ever wanted something where I could feel comfortable."

She looked away and nodded, mulling over the thought. Then she smiled. "Well, I hope we can both feel comfortable." She was looking at him then and her eyes spoke volumes.

They finished their hot dogs. By then, the sky was glowing and the lights were turning on. The paper holders for the hotdogs lay limp like carcasses.

#

In the car, their arms were entangled and her hair was spilling onto his shoulders. They could both smell the hot dogs on each other's breath. Her mouth was wet and she had a forcefulness to her. Seth thought it was like a pent-up surge of water, released as a dam broke. She was pure energy.

Then they separated, both basking in the break from each other. She turned to him with an inquisitive thing in her eyes. "Do you ever think about choices?"

"How d'you mean?"

"Just, like, choices. I chose to be here with you. I chose to leave that convent. Now we can, like, go forward." She'd separated from him a bit, and moved her hands like a teacher, speaking in a clear, lucid manner.

He thought about that. He ran a hand down her arm until he found her hand. Their fingers clasped like puzzle pieces. "I chose not to go back home."

"Chicago's your home, then? Not here?" Her eyes were unblinking and clear, like mirrors. He looked slightly to the side.

He chuckled. "Hell, I don't even know where home is."

They were silent and could hear the buzzing of the cicadas and the deep, mechanical hum of far-off traffic behind them. She rubbed his knuckles with her fingertips in a way he thought was sexy. He turned in his seat and leaned to kiss her. "You feel good."

She blushed. "Oh, shit, you're just too nice, aren't you?"

"Impossible." He leaned back against his seat. She put a hand on his shoulder and ran it slowly down his arm.

"So, what's next? You going to just fuck me and go?" She had that mischievous grin again. She had a way of winding him up. Of saying the thing that could spur something else, some new doorway entirely.

He laughed. He put a hand on her belly. "I'm not going anywhere."

She checked her phone in her bag on the floor of the car, and gave him a look again, slightly guilty. "Well, about that…"

\#

It was nothing personal, she said. It was just that the children were coming back at 11:00 and they wouldn't know what to make of him. Soon, she said. They just needed a little more time, she said, to truly adjust to the world outside. Seth was surprised that he didn't really have a feeling about the children at all.

So he dropped her at her place. It was a narrow, forest-green garage behind a larger two-story white stucco house. The lights in the house were off and there was a red Infinity parked there, next to her Acura. She turned back and kissed him long and hard on the lips, and then she was gone— a sliver growing tinier in the dark. Then a warm light turned on in the distance in the garage.

\#

And he was wired after that. He couldn't rest, so when he got back to the trailer, he turned off his car and started to walk. His camera was in the bag in his room and he'd not even touched it in weeks.

There was a little breeze that blew through his hair, cooled his skin. He thought about a plane. It wasn't an unfamiliar thing to him. The world had taken him to Colorado for a year, where he'd tried his hand at substitute teaching, and then to Washington State, where he'd written for a little while for an alt weekly about politics and the environment. It was in his blood to keep going. He got bored easily. He'd wondered often if he was just ADHD, or one of those other splintered, ever-evolving diagnoses. He'd never been tested. His mother had once off-handedly admitted that she didn't believe in vaccines, so that explained much of how his childhood had gone.

And he'd had all these jobs, but none of them seemed to stick. He only thought of them as ways to pass the time. That was all it was. Passing time.

\#

She told him to come over and they watched a movie on her couch, a thriller where a cop in a long coat felt like he was going mad.

"Hey, why don't you tell me about your kids, anyway? I never seem to hear about 'em."

The glow of the TV was white and blue on her slender face, which was widening into a smile. "Well, today Micah swam in the river for almost an hour. He's getting so good. And the seven-year-old, David, he's reading so well. It seems like not long ago I was having to help him sound out words."

"They're veritable prodigies."

She giggled. "They're so smart. They'll make me feel stupid soon."

"Ah, but you're resourceful. You escaped a cult."

She got a thoughtful look about her. "True. But they might be able to do that, too."

"You ought to test that. Put 'em in, like, a boarding school."

She tapped her chin with her index finger. "I guess I'll have to put them in school. Summer'll be over before we know it."

Her finger was tracing his arm. She was closer to him than he remembered. He looked in her eyes. "Oh. You ready, then?"

She was on top of him then. He couldn't see the TV and it didn't matter anymore.

\#

> **" The cruelty of the man. Seth thought the deep South had such a peculiar breed of insanity to it— such an insular evil.**

After, as they lay on the couch, her voice came up with the question, ghostly and soft like vapor rising. "How many girls have you been with?"

He shifted to prop his head on his elbow and look at her. "Uh, there was Alex, from school, who, I dunno, we just sat together. And there was Theresa, in college. She was real smart. I mean, I guess those were the main ones."

"Were there others?" She was smiling at him, ear to ear, her chin on his chest. "Are you a storied repertoire of steamy past loves?"

Seth just shrugged. "A few things, here and there. Nothing serious, you know."

And that was when the tone shifted. It was something in the air, he thought. Like a storm was coming.

The movie was still on, the volume a low, dull drone of a hum. Stella shifted in his arms and she wasn't looking at him so much as at the ceiling. He looked up. It was a plain, stucco white ceiling.

"Everything alright?"

She said, "I'm just thinking."

The movie was nearing its end. She disengaged herself from him and started pulling her clothes back on.

"What's wrong?" He sat up on the couch, feeling the vibe die.

"Nothing. Just cold's, all." She was pulling on her skirt at a rapid clip. Then her shirt, buttoning it up.

She wasn't looking at him. She adjusted her shirt. "I dunno. It's not you. Not really. But it's the idea of it. Of people just being out here and doing whatever they want, just... sleeping with whoever. I can't fathom it. I know, logically, that it's fine, but I can't get used to it. It's all the sounds and the sights and the tastes of everything around here, really, not just that. It's wild to me."

Her back was to him. She was trembling a little.

He put his hand right in the center of her back. "I don't mind that. I can help you."

She shook her head. "It's hard for anyone to be inside anyone else's mind."

\#

The guy with the big beard came into town after that. There were murmurs of this at Shanahan's. Abe Robinson was big-bellied and he'd carved out his own little corner of Shanahan's with Buck and Tim, also old 50-somethings living out their days. Abe was the loudest of them, with his braying, nasal voice carrying over the bar like a shitting seagull. "You know, that man was at the market. Mrs. Martin said he was buying pornographic titles. She said he gave her a mean look when they were leaving. Said he seemed like a troublemaker."

Seth doubted this was true. He wouldn't have said a word most nights, but that night he was four whiskeys deep and working on a fifth.

So he stood in front of their table. "Abe, you beat your wife into a coma once. I remember that. You judge other people now?" Seth felt a hot, hazy surge in his throat, and his fists had their own life now.

Abe stood up. He had a crazy grin on his face, lips peeled back like a devil's face. "Boy, you shouldn't speak about shit you don't know. Your mama, she knew that. Your mama was a good old girl. Didn't go off half-cocked, tryin' to forget where she came from."

Seth was seeing double now. "Fuck you, you racist cocksucker." He was turning to go when the glass flew like a bullet and clipped him on the side of the forehead. He felt a white-hot searing sensation, and then his cheek was against the floor.

\#

"You're gonna need stitches." The ER doctor was middle-aged and thin, with a bald spot and a somber look behind thick glasses.

"Well, fuck." He'd gotten a decent look at himself. He was OK, but the side of his forehead was deeply cut, swathes of angry red like sunspots.

The ER doctor walked off to get his equipment. Stella was sitting on the chair, her hands clasped in her lap. "So you think you're OK?"

He nodded. "Thanks for coming." He pressed the ice pack to his head. The face of Abe lingered in his mind. The cruelty of the man. Seth thought the deep South had such a peculiar breed of insanity to it— such an insular evil.

The doctor came back.

"I'm never good watching, like, medical stuff," she said. And she turned back to her phone. Her fingers were moving too fast, and trembling a bit.

\#

Later, she told him about the bearded man. It was all coming full circle. It was what he had suspected the whole time; the fire that had lit his bloody bar confrontation. They sat in his car, barely lit except by one dim far-off street-light that cast them both in dirty orange.

"His name's Judah," she said, her voice quiet. "He wants to… well, talk, about the way we left things."

"Talk." Seth had a hand over hers. He ran his fingers over her knuckles.

"He called me yesterday, and we had a conversation for maybe 10 minutes? And he seemed, like, genuinely sorry."

"You told me he was… well, commanding. Did he threaten you?"

She shook her head. "He was telling me he knows that was wrong."

"That's what all these guys say. I knew a girl once, up in Colorado… her husband would try and, you know, manipulate her in some way…"

She thought about it and shook her head. "He seemed genuine to me."

Seth leaned back against the seat. "So what do you want to do?" He was putting together the pieces. In the bar, he'd known this was coming, like a dog with a storm. It was the feeling beyond words or reason.

She was mostly cast in shadow now. "I don't know. I'm still thinking. I definitely don't want to go back to the convent… but the thing is, Judah, he says we don't have to. He says we can stay down here or go somewhere else. He just, like, wants to be near the kids."

For now, Seth thought, but he didn't say that. He thought about Stella and her children and couldn't put together a full picture. He couldn't reconcile the family with this woman before him.

#

They didn't see each other for a few days and he got a text from a buddy, Eric Tseng, who told him to drive to Orlando for a visit. Eric was a big social media marketing guru who knew everyone. In school, he'd been annoyingly positive and had been able to walk into any room and strike up a conversation no matter what. Now he worked for Universal as some type of press-release-generator. Seth would log onto Facebook every few days and see him pimping something.

So he drove up the winding, tree-laden highway, the sun beating through his windshield, and he reached the winding metropolis of Disney with its towering hotels, the traffic metal and screaming like a giant machine full of cogs.

Starbucks was lit up with people on their phones, reading books, conversing with friends in a chatter that formed a sort of white noise all around him. At the counter, he ordered a coffee. Eric was sitting by the wall. He was a twitchy kind of guy who always seemed to be virulently awake, always on his phone, and he wore tight collared shirts and skinny jeans so constricting they looked to cut off circulation. "So, you made it, I see."

Seth took a seat, placing his coffee on the table. "Ah, yeah, it's an hour and a half drive."

Eric was leaning in, talking fast and low, as if it were some criminal conspiracy.. "I've been talking with some guys in southern France. You remember Jim from college?"

Seth had a vague recollection of a tall, jockish guy with a boyish face.

"Sure, I guess."

"Yeah. Him and this team of scientists are trying to, you know, look at the effects of climate change there, on wine and all the farming and all that? And I was thinking you'd be good for it." Eric sipped a steaming Starbucks cup. "It's just, like, a cool thing and you'd be researching and taking pictures and whatnot. It's a part time thing, but you know, it pays well."

Seth nodded. He thought of Stella and their nights together. Then he thought of the French countryside. Of driving on weekends and sipping expensive wine and champagne with those views. Of the glistening plains. "Hey, that sounds awesome, man." His voice sounded far away, and he wondered if it came off disconnected somehow, aloof.

Eric always had a glimmer in his eye when making plans, like an engine going at full speed. "Can I tell 'em you're in?"

Seth cleared his throat. "Uh, let me get back to you. It's just... I need to sort some things out still, with my mom's place."

#

He drove back with the glut of possibility growing pregnant in his head, drunk on it, living outside himself almost. The road was dark. Trees stretched out like winding labyrinths and the darkness sank through his head like a stone through water.

His first girlfriend, Alex, had been as dirt-poor as him. Both of them in identical shitty trailers, with her father, a tax-dodger, and her mother, a ferocious drunk— the kind of person liable to start a fight, to break glasses and plates. Alex, as a result, spent a lot of time just wandering, and he had wandered with her for years in his teens.

Then there was his second girlfriend, Theresa, who had seemed straight-laced and smart. She'd majored in finance and all, a skinny preppy girl who'd lit up the room when she walked in, who could engage you on politics or movies or whatever. Then he found out she was a kleptomaniac who was stealing jewelry or checks from her roommates and hall-mates. It felt so odd to have spent all those afternoons and nights with her, then, after he knew. There had been a whole email from the administration and everything.

The common thread was that there was no real longevity. They'd passed through his life like trains, bound for other horizons.

    #

Seth sat on the outside patio at the coffee shop with his steaming coffee. The waitress, a skinny 19-year-old with her bangs tinged a bright violet, brought him a bagel.

Then Stella was coming up. She leaned down and kissed him on the lips.

After she'd come back with her own coffee, and she sat before him prim and put together like a painting. He wondered how women could do that, just look so put together. Then he supposed it wasn't all of them. "It feels nice out today, doesn't it?"

He opened his mouth and then closed it. He looked at the coffee. It rippled in the air. "A buddy of mine, the other day, told me there's a job in Paris I could have. I'm thinking about it."

Her expression changed. Now she was perked up, full of wonder. "Oh, Paris sounds lovely."

"I'd love to take you there," he said.

She had a big grin and a blush, like the sun coming out from behind a cloud. "We wouldn't be able to enjoy the view. We'd be too busy in bed."

He laughed. "Hell, I'd never let you go."

They drank their coffee. Stella looked down at hers, brow furrowed.

Seth said, "Your coffee making you sad? Want me to beat it up?"

Her laugh wasn't as mirthful as it should've been he thought. She looked up at him, shyly, but then cast her eyes down. She sipped her coffee. "I guess that's a bit of a longshot dream."

He nodded. He felt like he'd been doused with cold water. "Yeah, yeah. But maybe..."

The way she looked at him then, she seemed to have aged a decade. Her eyes had a reproachful look and seemed to contain multitudes, all sadness and hope and dreams yanked away.

    #

He took her grocery shopping with him. "I want to see what you're like every day," she said.

So they were lost in the maze of white, speckled tile, frozen foods, boxes of snacks and books you'd find at the airport. There was a sanitized air and an 80s pop song playing over the speakers at a low whisper. People crossed in front of one another wielding baskets and pushing creaking carts.

He picked out a loaf of bread, loaded it in the cart. "So, is this everything you dreamed of?"

She trailed behind him, examining the aisles. "It's whimsical."

He chuckled. He picked out a jar of peanuts and added it to the cart. "Glad I could make it happen for you."

In the next aisle over, she plucked a bag of frozen broccoli from the freezer. "Why not get some healthy stuff in there?"

He smiled at her, but picked it back up from the cart and moved it back to the freezer. The freezer door slammed with a clap. The cool air, like mist, lingered anyway. Her brow wrinkled. "What's that for? Can't take suggestions from a girl, huh?"

He chuckled. "Nah, it's just… don't need stuff for the freezer, since I don't know how long I'm staying."

"Surely a mantra that will lead to greater health."

But when he looked back at her, she was walking with her arms crossed. Her face, always so open to emotion, was turned down, a cloud over her. He said, "Hey, what's wrong? Did that bother you just now?"

He picked up a bag of wheat corn chips, put it in the basket.

She walked up closer to him. "Well, so what? You're just going to go, like that? You decided already?"

He felt a stone sink in his gut. Shit. "I dunno, babe. I was just going to do what I've always done."

"You're a man with no home." She didn't say this in a pithy way. But her tone, thoughtful and airy, as if rolling the concept over in her mind and studying it, somehow made him feel worse. He thought of her own life, which seemed the exact opposite of his.

"I guess so."

She flipped her curly hair back over her shoulder. "I envy you, you know. That you can just pick up and go. I just wish you'd told me up front…" She stopped and knelt down, picked out a bag of apple chips. "I always like these."

Seth kept going with the cart, feeling the wheels and the rust of the thing, hearing it creak and feeling like everyone could hear it. He didn't want everyone to hear that racket.

Stella rubbed her arms with her own hands like she was cold.

Seth said, "Babe, I just… you know I didn't mean…"

But they were coming to the cash register. He had barely noticed. The lady at the register was craggy-faced, her skin worn by the sun. She eyed Seth with a death stare. "You coming today?"

Seth began putting his items on the moving treadmill.

\#

In the car, the sun shone on the dusty, smudged glass of his windshield. Her seatbelt clicked as she put it into the holder. He said, "Look, you know, I just didn't know what I was doing. It all happened so fast."

She looked at him with a sort of analytical glance. But she didn't say anything.

He put the key into the ignition and started to drive. He spoke again, even though his gut was telling him to shut up for once. "And, hey, you haven't told me whether you're getting back with that guy yet. I don't know what you're doing, either."

She scoffed. "It's my fault, then?"

"Not your fault. Just saying, we're both kinda in transit, you know? One thing led to another."

He was driving through traffic, passing by the rows of the Hummers, the Buicks, the rusted old trucks. They were turning onto the smaller street that led back to her place, the sort of modest suburban abode, with its houses all set up on a grid, all of them with perfectly trimmed grass at the behest of a homeowners' association.

She tapped her chin as she did when thinking. She wasn't looking at him. "We're like pinballs. Just… thrown around. Like the game we played, that first date, remember?"

"Yeah, I remember." He pulled into her driveway. He stopped and put the car in park.

She undid her seatbelt and then looked at him again. She had a way of it. Of these long, surreal, probing glances, like hypnosis. Then she leaned forward with a startling kind of quickness and embraced him in a deep hug, patting his back, and then she kissed him chastely on the lips as she got out. There were no words exchanged and he left in a kind of daze.

It reminded him, as he drove away, of his first kiss. It had been with Alex. They were 15 and both decided not to go to the freshman dance, thinking it uncool. They'd instead walked around the neighborhood, the trees providing shade, talking about Green Day and AFI and Marilyn Manson. Edgy shit. They both agreed never to give into the mainstream corporate trends. To never work in an office. It was in that kind of a mind-meld that he stopped her on the side of the road, autumn leaves crunching beneath their Reeboks, and kissed her on the lips. Her lips had been soft and cool and they'd both been surprised, but then deeper in them, it had made sense. But he didn't know what had happened to her after school had finished. They'd walked across a stage one April, years later, and had drifted apart like sand through fingers.

\#

He texted Eric Tseng at a stop light: Hey man I'm in for France. Let's do this thing.

But after that, he felt a twitch in his gut, a churning. And when he tried to go to sleep, he ended up twisting and turning all night. He woke up every two hours, checked his phone, saw no text messages and also that it was some ungodly hour, feeling the weariness in his eyes and his bones. He knew he'd pay the next day.

\#

It turned out he was right, for the following day, everything seemed to irritate him. The light was too bright and he couldn't seem to make himself comfortable. He got an omelet at a diner near his place; a small tin shack by the road and you were serenaded with the roar of trucks, the uncouth banter of the truckers, the smell of gas and oil and cheese. Inside, it was all weather-beaten tiles and grease stains on the tables. His waitress was Millie, the owner, now in her 60s and still fighting tooth and nail. Millie patted his shoulder, told him "we're all so sorry to hear about your mother."

But the food was good. Seth had always held to this – that the food at places like this was something you couldn't find anywhere else.

His phone buzzed on the table, indicating a text, and he hated how his heart palpitated then. It was like he was a kid in school, pining over someone to go to a stupid dance with. Sweat on his hands, he turned over his phone too quick, almost dropping it, but catching it at the last second.. The text was an automated one, asking him to pay his phone bill on the 12th. The coffee was getting cold, and he picked up the mug and chugged it down, a race against the temperature.

#

One day, when he was 16, his mother had come back home after a day of shopping and she was bubbly, happy and sober. It was so unusual that, as he was sitting there playing Street Fighter to whittle away the hours, he briefly wondered if she'd been replaced by some alien, some body-snatcher. She was putting the groceries in the fridge and in the cabinets, all vegetables and chips and frozen meats, and telling him she wanted to drive up to the coast. "It'll be fun," she said. "I know we haven't done anything fun in a while."

And he was thinking about Alex back then, and didn't have the heart to tell his mother that he was looking forward more to sitting on a couch in the dark with Alex, watching old movies and not really watching them.

But it would not come to pass, this ephemeral coast-trip— it was the thing of ghosts. He came home the next day and found her with a half-empty bottle of wine on the table, slumped over, her cheek against the surface, level with the wine glass. Her boyfriend of the month had blown town with a stripper. This seemed cliché, but in the small Crescent City of the late 90s, it was just part and parcel.

"It's all fucked," she told him, her voice slurred with the wine and the even more intangible deep-rooted despair which Seth would come to believe was just deep-rooted in people, you couldn't get it out. "You try and love people and they just spit in your face. Don't trust people, son."

Seth hadn't really taken it to heart. Who thought about love at 16?

He sat now in his mother's house on her couch and could see the table where he found her that day, 15 years previous. He could see his mother's fallen leg lamp from A Christmas Story by the door, the ashtray and the fallen poster of Prince in the corner and the coffee table, with its numerous magazines and books falling around it like a dilapidated temple. The whiskey stains on the carpet were permanent and, if one's nasal passages were perfectly clear, you could still smell the whiskey.

He saw the area of the wall, halfway through the hallway back to the bedrooms and bathroom, where a boyfriend of hers had punched a hole – he and his mother had to spend a Saturday morning with plaster and paint, trying to make it blend. But it wouldn't blend, not really. It just looked like a poorly-patched-up wall. Seth wasn't religious, but he'd thanked some deity somewhere when his mother had kicked that boyfriend, a local mechanic named Chad with a reputation for boozing and fighting, to the curb. He'd never hit either of them, but came perilously close every day, it seemed; it had lived in his eyes and his veins like poison.

He thought of all these old things and looked at the shadowy dilapidated ruin. This wasn't anything anymore. There was no future where he stayed here. He had to keep moving or die. She finally texted him that night as he was going to bed. Her text was short: Can we talk in person tomorrow?

#

They met by the lake where they'd walked that first night, with the crisp morning air and the gunmetal gray sky. She wore a light pink cardigan over a white T-shirt and dark jeans, and the look, the combination of all of it, began to tug strings in him, made him want to take her in his arms. This feeling came on like a high, and he shook his head and pushed it back down.

They walked for a little while, and she told him about her last few days, about her kids. "They're really getting used to it here. I think staying will be quite nice for them. They're making friends around the neighborhood and everything. It's so weird, like… it's almost a normal life, which is so weird for me to have."

He put a hand on her shoulder and squeezed, felt the softness of her clothes.. "Well, you're out there doing it. That's amazing."

She smiled, but pulled away from him. "So, I guess we ought to talk about all of it…"

Seth put his hands in his pockets to stop the trembling. "Maybe we do, huh?"

She nodded. "So, I guess I'll just say it. Do you even want kids? Do you want to take care of them?"

He looked at the sky and felt his mouth dry, felt his seasonal allergies flaring up. He opened his mouth to talk and didn't know what to say.

She put her hand on his arm and didn't wait for him. "It's been, I don't know, like a dream. Like we've been going through some great wondrous funhouse. I always wanted to do this. Just get lost with somebody. Do you know how many times I fantasized about this in the convent? Lying there and wishing I could go see the world?"

Seth nodded. "I'm glad I could do that for you."

They walked to the bench a few feet ahead of them and sat down, not touching. She kept her hands in her lap, prim, and he put an arm over the back of the bench.

She was clearing her throat, shifting her hair over her shoulder with one palm. "But now I'm feeling this pull. Like I've seen the real consequence. A dream's never the same when you think about the next day and the day after." She was talking faster now, as if some nervousness had come over her in a wave. "My kids ask me if we're staying here, and I don't know what to tell them. Everything is confusing right now."

"The pinball thing. What you'd said before." He took a hand out of his pocket and smoothed his hair back.

"Yeah." She wasn't looking directly in his eyes. Like he was the sun.

"I mean, yeah, you know? I don't know what I'd do with kids. Hell, I can't picture it." He stepped back and let the breeze from the lake caress him. He felt a weight off him, saying all of this.

"It's tough. It's a lot of stuff. It's all the time." She was looking at the lake now. A family of ducks congregated at the banks, bickering among one another.

Seth sighed. "Well, this isn't the best date I've had." He let his hands fall to his sides, lank and limp.

She chuckled and looked at him, a small, wry smile spreading over her face. "I didn't think it would be."

"Would be weird if it was, I guess."

He looked at her. She was looking down at her fingernails, turning her hand as if it contained patterns and swirls unknown to him. He said, "You can go, you know. I suppose we both ought to."

She looked back at him with a sad, apologetic kind of smile. "We can just sit for a while."

"Okay, then."

Behind them, the bustle of traffic raged, and before them the lake was still, except for the ducks' movements, creating tiny inconsistent ripples.

*

THE MESS OF IT
A POST-GREAT WAR TALE OF THE A
READ NOW @ PATREON.COM/THEMESSO

"The Mess of It All" is an episodic, pulpy serial adventure, told through the journals of an amateur anthropologist of sorts- Ernest Freeborne- a young man navigating the Wasteland which was once the United States of America.

An alternate history will unfold as Ernest wanders the Dieselpunk, Post Apocalyptic Wastes, speaking with survivors of The Great War and The Disaster of '21, reading old journals and records, and getting tangled up in dangerous encounters on the way.

A strange new history waits to be told, while the strange new era demands to be understood.

no one will sit by my side on my last day

and say i never outran lightning

no one will hear those words

never not once

i find great solace and pride in knowing that i will spend most of life

living faster than lightning strikes

even the moments when i slow

to catch my breath a little

when the hair on my neck begins to rise

a little

even when the soil and sky

hold hands charging through me

still that will be victory ... if

having enticed the heavens and earth

to make their way through this body

i survive

SUNRISE
BY COLE REEVES

sunrise

I remember
dawn
her soft footsteps
climbing heaven's hill

on her walk back from the well
holding a cup of god in her hand

how she poured it, slow
and soft, like the first note of a hymn

and how
I drank like a man rescued
at sea

as she went to fill her pail again

THE HOUSE ALWAYS WINS
BY COOPER NICKERSON

The Governor had waited for sixty years

for the coming of the Gliese 581 star system. Finally, its sun had come into view through a large circular porthole in his cavernous quarters. Gliese's sun looked like a tiny, lonely ember sitting on a bed of black coal, glowing feebly. It was the most noticeable star of all the nearby star systems because its mass was three times that of Earth's sun. One of the planets, Gliese G, would soon be the Governor's new home.

The ship wide speaker barked: "This is Captain Foster. We are approaching the outer vicinity of the Gliese system. In order to exit safely, we will engage a gradual braking system in an hour's time. Don't be alarmed by a sudden change in the motion of the ship. This is a normal reaction. The braking will run its course for a few days, and then we will arrive at Gliese G. Thank you for your attention." There were over a quarter of a million people celebrating on all decks of the five-kilometer long generational ship.

The Governor wanted to burst into applause, but didn't because there wasn't anyone in his quarters to share in his celebration. He was a bachelor through and through, though he had someone in mind that he wanted to marry and raise his children with. He had planned his announcement after he had settled on a new planet.

The Governor was a burly man with a salt and pepper mane, and a deep tan from his frequent use of the tanning bed. He was dressed in an ankle length gray robe with red cuffs and a scarf. His arms were folded squarely on his barrel chest as he admired the view of the sun. He was extremely happy. He retreated two steps and the back of his legs touched the high back armchair. He sat down, grunted quietly, and continued looking at the red sun.

He was anxious about the new home. He had never set foot on a planet before because he had been born on the ship. He wondered what would happen to him when he stepped into the strange new world. Would he feel the change of gravity? Feel lighter or heavier? He had wondered about the planet's air, too. Would his lungs feel different when he inhaled it? There were so many questions he wanted answers to: What would happen to him when he started to make a living in the new world? Would he like it or not? These questions made him feel nervous, but with his feet on the floor, he felt the steady humming of the ship's engines which gave him a bit of comfort. The ship had been his home all his life. He remembered back when he was a boy, only taking his first step into what became the journey of his manhood. His father, a Governor at the time, showed him the ship's enormous engines for the first time. His father told him that his first responsibility started there because the engines were the lifeline to their new world. He also remembered when his grandfather, a former Governor too, told him that—

An intercom buzzed.

The Governor grumbled and got up. He rounded the chair and headed for the desk. He tapped the panel. "Yes?"

"Governor, you are wanted in the sickbay," a voice said abruptly.

The Governor blinked, puzzled at the line of the request. "I am sorry…whom am I speaking to?"

A long pause from the intercom, and then someone spoke. "My apologies, sir. This is First Officer Wang from the bridge. You are wanted at the infirmary."

"Sickbay?"

"Yes, sir."

The Governor stopped long enough to gather his thoughts. Why am I needed at the sickbay? My last check-up was a month ago. I passed with flying colours. What is the urgency? "Could you please tell me why I am needed at the sickbay?"

Another pause. "Uh, I am not sure exactly," the first officer said with discomfort in his voice. "Chief medical officer insisted you come to the sickbay."

"Chief medical officer insisted? Why?"

"I don't know, but the captain will meet you there, too. I am just following orders. Sorry, sir."

The Governor inhaled and held his breath for a moment. He understood the chain of command. He exhaled gently and said, "All right, I'll meet… at the sickbay."

"Very good, sir. We are sending someone to pick you up in about two minutes.”

“All right. Thanks.”

The Governor clicked the intercom off, muttered silently to himself, and wondered why he was needed at the sickbay. Was there someone there that I might know who was sick or injured? My brother? My sister? Aunts? Uncles? Mama? Papa died a few years ago. So did my grandparents. Surely one of my relatives would have called me, but they haven’t. Who would want me there? I can’t even come up with the name of the person wanting me at the sickbay.

The Governor paced anxiously around his quarters as if searching for something important to take with him— a purse or a journal, maybe. Finally, he headed for the round door and stopped. He turned his head and frowned at his room, at the big porthole, and at the distant red sun. He wanted to stay and watch the sun grow bigger as the ship approached it, but...

“Humph,” he sighed resignedly. “Sickbay, it is.”

The Governor pressed a button beside the door. The door opened like an eye expanding its iris. The three guardsmen spun about, startled.

“Sir?” the lead guard said. “I wasn’t aware of the schedule—“

“Yes, yes, I know.” The Governor waved his hand. “I am needed at the sickbay.”

“Sickbay? Are you ill, sir?”

“No, no. I am fine. I got a call from the bridge. They want me there now.”

“You will need a transport. I’ll call up one of my men.”

“It has been taken care of.”

“Oh? Then you need an escort. I’ll come with you.”

“Fine with me,” the Governor said, stepping out of the doorway. One of the guardsmen volunteered to close the door.

The Governor looked up and down the tubular corridor, waiting. His corridor was one of many streets. He greeted people as they walked by him, smiling and nodding. After a minute, a small car without a top appeared. The driver was a young dark man and he braked.

“I am Yeoman Singh. I am here to deliver you to the infirmary,” the driver said.

“He is with me.” The Governor indicated the lead guard.

The driver nodded in acknowledgment. The Governor sat in the front and the lead guard hopped in the back.

"Let's go," the Governor said, waving his hand impatiently. He wanted to come back as soon as possible to watch the red sun.

The three men sped through the various innards of the colossal ship and arrived at the infirmary a short time later. A woman in a peach-colored jumpsuit watched the Governor and his lead guard walk into the center. He turned to the lead guard.

"I'll go alone," the Governor said.

"Sir?" The lead guard looked troubled, as he didn't want the Governor to go without security.

"I'll be all right," the Governor said with an assured blink.

The lead guard gazed at the woman, and then back to the Governor. He sighed with reluctance. "Fine, sir. I'll be waiting for you."

"Good," the Governor nodded and turned to the woman.

The woman, with a nervous look, nodded. "I have been expecting you, Governor."

"Are you the doctor?"

"No," the woman said. "Please follow me."

The Governor inhaled, as if exasperated, and said, "Lead on."

They went inside the infirmary. The reception, the halls, and the surgery room were bright, clean and white. There were no patients around because everyone onboard the ship was relatively healthy, due to constant biomonitors check-ups. There were a couple of doctors, and some nurses, milling about as if to keep themselves busy, or to be available for any unforeseeable emergencies, however little they may be.

"Where are we going?" the Governor asked.

"We are here." The woman glanced meaningfully at a couple of people standing by the glassed partition of the birthing center. It was Captain Foster talking to a woman. The Governor looked puzzled. Why the birthing center? What is so important that I had to come here? They had better explain something, or else I am heading back to my quarter.

"Captain," the Governor nodded with a mixture of patience and a luminous smile.

"Governor," the captain nodded. He was forty years old with gray bristle brush hair. He was dressed in a white military outfit. "This is Doctor Honeycutt, the chief medical officer."

"Governor." Doctor Honeycutt's face erupted in a cautious smile. She was nervous. She had never met a person of the Governor's status. She was twenty-nine and wore a light blue jumpsuit. She was the youngest chief medical officer onboard.

There was a moment of awkward pause as she was unsure how to begin this conversation.

"So, why is it you want me here today?" The Governor frowned with curiosity.

"Doctor?" Captain Foster turned to the doctor.

"Hmm, I don't know exactly how to explain this to you." Doctor Honeycutt smoothed her ponytail that shone like fiber-optics, and she blinked her crystal blue eyes. She was still nervous. "Something miraculous took place a few moments ago."

The Governor nodded, listening.

"A baby boy was born."

"Surely, this is a miracle," the Governor said.

"Yes, Your Excellency, but," the doctor paused, trying to gather a thought to find the right words, "the baby has an auditory failure."

The Governor stared at her with a look of loss. "I don't understand. What are you saying?"

"What I am saying is that the baby was born normal, and, at some point, became deaf."

The Governor was shocked because there hadn't been any deaf babies born on the ship for generations. Nor had there been any blind or crippled.

"Deaf, you say?" asked the Governor.

"Yes, I don't expect you to understand, or believe, but he really is deaf."

"Let me guess, you deliberately let the child grow inside the mother's womb and delivered it without intervention?"

"Oh, no, no, Your Excellency. I wouldn't think of that," Doctor Honeycutt said.

"How is this possible? Did you do the screening before it matured into a full-grown?"

"Yes, yes. We did follow every procedure laid out by the Convention on Prevention of Disablement. I don't know why it happened, but it did."

"It just happened? Surely you must have noticed the imperfection before full development took place."

"We monitored the baby from the beginning of conception and didn't see anything related to imperfection."

"And...?"

"After the birth, we checked his health, looking for any flaws. We found none, but then, after a couple of hours, we found the baby's auditory organs had somehow deteriorated."

"It turned deaf on its own?" The Governor looked incredulous. "How?"

"I don't know. We tried to come up with an explanation for that. It could be some kind of auditory organ biochemical breakdown. But I assure you we are working on the cause."

The Governor looked at Captain Foster, wondering if the captain believed her story.

Then he looked back at the doctor. "Where is the child?"

"Over there." Doctor Honeycutt pointed through the glass-partition to the lone, white bassinet inside the neonatal room.

The Governor didn't move. Instead he looked at the baby wrapped in a white blanket, whining and fussing. He had seen the birth and growth of so many babies in his lifetime. He had overseen a strict manipulation on genetic hygiene, and handled, but never watched, the extermination of unborn babies with undesired handicaps and other disabilities. These practices were attributed to the fact that the ship couldn't afford to provide any kind of handicap services during the long voyage to the new home. The mission couldn't afford to provide them with the physical, auditory, and ocular implants necessary to make their handicapped lives more comfortable and accessible. It wasn't about discrimination or cruelty, it was about maintaining the population of the ship, to prevent it from bursting at seams, so to speak.

"I know a rule has been broken," the doctor said. "But it wasn't... intentional. We can't really undo what has been done."

The Governor said, quietly, "It is an unfortunate situation."

"Yes, and I want you to spare the child until we get to the planet," the doctor suggested.

The Governor stared at the doctor. "What?" he whispered.

Doctor Honeycutt forced herself to go on, "We have to face the fact, illogical as it may sound. I can repair the baby's hearing. The baby will survive once we have established a colony on the new planet."

The Governor continued to listen hesitantly.

"After the operation, we'll set up a service for the disabled people on the planet, and it would be the first of its kind."

The Governor suddenly liked the idea. "The first of a kind," he said, nodding slowly.

"Yes, it would be wonderful for the future children with disabilities. Your name will be heralded as the first Governor to implement such services."

The doctor's suggestion sounded good and promising, but it was hard for the Governor to process. He had never encountered this kind of situation before. His father had told him he had witnessed these "termination procedures" a few times in his lifetime. So did his grandfather. They told him they were an unpleasant experience, and hoped that he wouldn't have to experience one. The Governor turned to the captain who hadn't said a word.

"What do you think, Captain?" he asked.

"This is a difficult situation to make, sir," Captain Foster admitted.

"What would you do if you were in my shoes?"

The captain inhaled and said thoughtfully, "I would spare the child, but..."

"But what?"

"Well, as an officer of this ship, I would have to follow the protocol down to the very letter."

Doctor Honeycutt stepped in. "I agree with the captain, but, Governor, it is only for a few days. Let the baby live. No one has to know."

"Yes, you are right. No one has to know," the Governor said.

"We could put the baby in an isolated ward and have a limited supervised staff placed there on an hourly basis. It would be in total secrecy. You have my word on that."

The Governor sighed. He considered her suggestion. He looked up and down the empty hallway. He looked uncomfortable, as his legs were aching a bit, due to tiny, tiny, subtle increments of gravity plating over the years to get his body acclimated to the new planet's slightly heavier gravity. The doctor must have detected his discomfort. She crossed the hall and entered another room. She brought a chair out with her.

The Governor stared at the doctor for a moment and smiled inwardly.

"Thank you," he said, sitting down, grunting quietly.

"That's quite all right," the doctor said.

"All right." The Governor paused for a moment. "I am all ears, but make it brief, as I have other business to tend to." He wanted to get back to his quarters to look at the new sun as soon as possible.

The doctor cleared her throat, nervously. "I'll do my best."

"State your…case," the Governor said, as he began to massage his legs.

"Okay, but, first, let me say, thank you for your indulgence of allowing me to explain why I think the baby should live."

The Governor bowed his head. "Okay, no problem."

"I also hope I can help you understand why I don't want you to end the baby's life."

"Hmm." The Governor nodded.

"I know you are angry, or disappointed. I did what I thought was best."

> **The Governor sighed again. He felt his heart move after the doctor's emotional appeal. She was right, he thought, about not taking a life.**

The Governor continued to massage. .

"It isn't the baby's fault that it has this…this disability which followed his birth."

"Yes, I can understand that," the Governor said.

"Okay, look, Governor," the doctor interlaced her fingers as if begging, "as a doctor, as a physician, I cannot, in good conscience, employ such a practice to end a life. I would be violating the first and oldest oath I took as a physician – do no harm."

"Okay."

"We can work together, and look for anything that might help to save the baby's life. Think of what we could accomplish." A pause. "Like I said a moment ago, by doing this, we would advance the frontiers of medical services for disabled individuals in the new world. I have already outlined an entry that you and I will present to the colonization's first medical school. Our case would be a triumph. It has a nice ring to it, don't you think?"

"It sure does, but is that the best defense you can come up with, saving the baby's life?"

"I'll get into that, but, first, you must understand why I don't agree with the protocol."

The Governor frowned. "Why?"

"Because ending a life is unacceptable."

The Governor looked puzzled. "I don't understand."

"I know you, like me, are confronted with the dilemma of whether to follow the protocol, but, take my advice, it would be a waste of time to debate."

"Why would it be a waste of time?" the Governor asked.

"Because none of the protocols mention terminating a life, just a fetus."

Instantly, the Governor stopped massaging his leg. He looked surprised and troubled. He looked at the captain who was shaking his head downward, smiling subtly. He looked even more surprised than the Governor.

Slowly, the Governor turned to the doctor and gave her a long hard look. Ending a life is unacceptable. Hmm, she has been studying the protocol all along, he thought. He leaned back and said, "I see your point."

"That is precisely why I didn't want to terminate the baby's life, Governor," the doctor said, grimly.

The Governor nodded.

"Governor." The doctor made another step forward. "There is no one more qualified than you to make the right decision. I know you will make the right one, with the baby's future in mind. Spare the baby. Let him live, please," the doctor pleaded.

The Governor took a slow and deep sigh. He turned and looked up at the captain who had been very quiet the whole time. He looked down and massaged his aching legs. Then he stood, grunting, and looked out across the neonatal room.

The baby slept peacefully in his bassinet.

The Governor sighed again. He felt his heart move after the doctor's emotional appeal. She was right, he thought, about not taking a life. And she's right that it isn't the baby's fault. Not only that, but it will take some time for the People of Appeal to hear appeals from the judgements of the Colony Court and…indeed it would be a waste of time to debate, despite the fact we are only a few million miles away from our new home.

He turned around and took a couple of steps across the hall and stopped. He looked down at the floor and felt the braking machine of the ship bumbling subtly, setting itself into an imperceptible lurching motion. He wondered about the people and the children on the ship. What are they thinking about today? Are they excited about the new world? Are they happy? Will I be happy too?

He turned to the captain.

"Cap?"

"Yes?" The captain made one step forward.

"How long before we make landfall?"

"Oh, three or four months. Maybe more, considering the fact that we have to make some surveys for appropriate settlements. It could take months, as there may be other unforeseeable factors -"

"Okay, okay, I get it." The Governor waved a hand. He turned to the doctor who was waiting to hear his reply. She looked very anxious and hopeful. He sighed with regret.

"How many parents are expecting a child?" the Governor asked.

"Oh, I am not sure exactly how many –"

The doctor was cut off.

"Just give a conservative number."

"Umm, a couple thousand, maybe."

"Will any of them be born before the landfall?" he asked, his eyes squinting, listening intently.

"A few hundred, I think."

"Okay." The Governor put his hand against the wall, and pondered for a moment with the other hand on his beard. Then he looked at the doctor with arched eyebrows. "Let's say, hypothetically, I mean hypothetically, you understand?"

"Yes, Governor."

"Supposedly one or two babies happen to be born, like this baby here, with some sort of unexpected disability."

The doctor nodded, listening carefully.

"And we don't make landfall due to some unfortunate circumstances. And we have these... people with conditions to deal with. How do you propose we deal with them? What would happen if we continue to welcome the disabled? Let them live despite the protocol?"

The doctor paused, absorbed in thought.

"And the other thing is if, or when, the people find out that we have broken the law. What do you think will happen? Will they simply dismiss it?"

The doctor shook her head. "No."

"You see, the protocol, no matter how imperfect it is, exists for a reason: it is to ensure that the ship maintains a healthy and controlled population number. And, no matter what kind of circumstances we may encounter along the way, it is the only way to keep our society from... falling apart. Do you understand, Doctor?"

"Well, yes, but like you said, it is all hypothetical, and I doubt that we would ever encounter --"

"Oh, you are right." The Governor made a dismissive wave of hand. He turned around and walked briefly down the hall. He stopped and turned around. "I know it is just a hypothesis, but I have a job to do – that is to carry out the protocol like my father before me, and his father before him, and so on."

The doctor looked at him, saying nothing.

"Look." The Governor shook his head, sighing sympathetically. "I completely understand what you are trying to do, but if you were to ask me what I would do here, I could answer that."

"What is it?" The doctor asked.

"I would still choose to end the life of the child, for the sake of the ship. That is what I would do, Doctor."

The doctor reeled. "But why?"

"I'll tell you why. The baby is within the boundary of the ship and its law. I have no choice but to follow the law as it has been laid out for all of us on this ship."

"Even so close to the end of this journey?"

"Yes, even before the very end of the journey."

"Governor...the baby is alive --"

"How do you think it makes me feel? It is not an easy decision for me to make. I hate doing this, but I have a job to do. I have to follow the protocol. You, too, have a job, and I expected you to follow it." The Governor raised his eyebrows higher at the doctor.

"But the protocol specifically –"

"I have made my decision."

"But it is only for –"

"I am sorry. It is out of my hands."

"There is another option –"

"You said it would be a waste of time to debate. And I am not going to debate."

"Oh, I didn't mean that."

"Would you please carry out the order?" The Governor asked the doctor.

"Governor…"

"Are you refusing?"

"No, I am not. Just please think for a minute –"

"I will have you arrested for refusing an order."

The doctor went silent. There was a pause for a moment.

"Okay," the Governor said, almost out of breath. "If you can't do it. I'll find someone who can."

The doctor looked down, closing her eyes for a moment, and then she opened them up. She looked up to say. "That won't be necessary. I'll do it."

The Governor sighed with relief. "Very good, Doctor. Now, who are the parents?" he asked.

The doctor spoke uneasily. "The parents' names are Robert and Hilda Boucher. They are farmers."

"Do they know about this…abnormality?"

"No, I haven't told them."

"Anyone else know about this?"

"A couple of staff members, and a doctor from the birth."

"What are their names?"

The doctor looked troubled. "Why?"

"Just answer the question," the captain advised the doctor.

The doctor gulped her dry tongue and said, "It is nurse Schwartz and nurse Hempel, and Doctor Chen."

"Captain." The Governor turned. "You know what you have to do."

"Round them up, sir?"

"Yes."

"Very well, sir." The captain headed to an intercom on the wall in the hallway. He issued security details to someone from the police facility. He returned to the Governor. "Security will take care of them, sir."

The Governor nodded in acknowledgement. He turned to the doctor, who looked like she wanted to say something, but held back. "We can't have these people leaking this kind of information to the population. It would cause a massive protest, disrupting society while we near our new home. Do you understand?"

The doctor nodded.

"You can't tell anyone about this either."

"What about the parents? What should I tell them?"

The Governor inhaled sharply and said, "Tell them the child died."

"How can I – "

The Governor interrupted her. "Think of something."

The doctor looked at the captain and then back at the Governor. She sighed, "Okay."

"All right, I had better get back to my quarters. Is there anything else you want to say before I go?"

The doctor shook her head. The captain shook his, too.

"Report back to me when the…procedure is done, Captain."

"Will do, sir."

"Okay, then, good evening to you two."

"Same to you, sir," the captain replied.

The doctor just nodded.

Back to his quarters, the Governor sat in his armchair, feeling content to be where he was, watching Gliese's sun grow bigger by the minute. He was glad he didn't feel the discomfort his father and grandfather had often described feeling after ordering the brutal procedures. He hoped his guilty conscience would remain clear. He wanted to focus his attention on the new home planet, and plan out the preparation of colonization, and nothing more.

He spent a long moment thinking. "Ah," he said. "When I get married, I'll have a whole bunch of children, and it will not matter if one of them is born deaf or blind. I will set up a clinic for them, and I will fiercely protect my children against the planet's harsh wilderness…"

SHE WHO BURNS

BY GABRIEL MCLEOD

My Name is Doctor Alfred Lexington

and I fear my mind is changing. I know in my heart I have committed a terrible and frightening thing.

My master's degrees in parapsychology, mythology, sociology, and behavioral sciences prepared me not for the mysteries of life. I received my doctorate in theology, but it did not reveal the truth of what lies between heaven and hell. I have co-written a number of textbooks as well as having three of my own published and awarded in the Educational Research Review. My second piece, "Obsidian Shadows: Learning to Predict the Crimes of the Future by Studying the Evils of The Past" held two months on the nonfiction bestseller list. My words and thoughts will go down in history, and there are many professors and scholars who claim me as their inspiration. I am not trying to sound boastful— I am merely trying to establish that I once had a sound and scholarly mind.

I began research on what would have been my fourth book. It was to deal with the phenomenon of displaced spirits, or ghosts, as they are often called. In addition to ghosts, the book would address haunts, haints, orbs, will o' wisps, apparitions, frights, bogles, phantoms, shade, shadows, specters, eidolon, visitants, and wraiths. In other countries, they are known by myriad names. What I mean is, although the global definition of the so-called specter's form is universally known, they are not all the same. Whether it is an ectoplasmic imprint of the electrodes of a passed on human, the traumatized essence of someone whose life was taken away violently, or the lost, lone spirits trapped between the crossroad of life and afterlife. Whatever the explanation, there have been thousands of witnesses who have had a brief visit or sight of something from the beyond. None of them, however, can compare to the miraculous spectacle of "She Who Burns."

I was doing research for my book and interviewing various people who had seen or witnessed a physical abnormality. At the time, I had never seen one myself, though I was not skeptical of their existence. One thing all my studies had taught me was the possibility of any eventuality. There had been too many references throughout recorded history to have any doubt that these apparitions visited us from time to time. In fact, I was building another hypothesis on the "back stages" of reality where spirits traversed, possibly mute and ignorant of another, appearing and disappearing, like actors in and out of the wings of the theatre stage.

It had been three years of researching, flying to a small Irish town, where I witnessed an angry ghost who threw glass pints around a pub, and then to London, where I caught a passing glimpse of the Gentleman Ghost who strolled the alleys every fourth new moon. I flew across the pond back to the States where I traveled the South West to the Midwest, the North East back down to the Southern Belt where so many stories, so rich and full of detail, unfolded before me. I heard whispers from passing winds, saw floating balls of light rush down darkened corridors, saw imprints of a fearful face ethereally etched in a college window pane, I heard the weeping of the woman at the well, the late night walks of the lady in red, the sobbing of the boy under the bridge, and the moaning of the lady who cries beside the lake. They were always so fleeting, those shimmering glimpses of sad and lost beings.

It was invigorating and maddening trying to obtain viable information to document. I spoke to a witch from the backwoods of Mississippi who told me of spells and incantations to capture or summon a wandering spirit, but was warned against the dark arts and their possible aftereffects.

The majority of the tales involved some terrible moment of cruelty or injustice, or a moment of immeasurable grief or abandonment. Although there were some examples of unwarranted visitations or unexplainable other worldly lights, most occurrences did gravitate around a negative experience. Something so bad that the passing soul did not feel vindicated to the extent that it could not "shuffle off this too mortal coil." I buried myself deeper into my work, sleeping more during the daylight hours in order to create more time during the twilight, searching for my once seen spirits, listening to the ghostly murmuring of the newly and long deceased.

Perhaps it began from the inevitable confrontation of mortality, for I am now much older than the young man I once was. My full head of hair now replaced by wispy white strands, my tan skin replaced with brown liver spots and leathered lines. My eyes, once a brilliant bold blue, have faded like a spring afternoon to a light powdery blue and cannot see over five feet without the aid of glasses. I take very good care of myself, eating lightly with intakes of lots of vitamins, trying to be very cautious of my health. But the spring in my step has calmed, and the joints in my body tend to creak like rusty hinges.

Every man or woman confronts the concept of his or her mortality at one time or another and that time had reached me. I desperately grasped the spiritual phenomena as perhaps a way to unlock some arcane knowledge on death's door and perhaps understand better what could happen to me when that time came. From these thoughts began my idea for the fourth book. The grant was provided before I finished my proposal.

Gathering close to three years of field research on such gravely morbid material, I was beginning to feel haunted by my own soul— a soul chained to a man driven mad by the search for knowledge. The years behind were facing me with their pockets empty of justifications.

There were hotels and parking lots, homes and cemeteries, restaurants and toilets, all who claimed to be haunted. Three fourths of them actually were, but only one fourth did I actually have the opportunity to witness, sometimes visiting for a day, sometimes camping out for a week. Oftentimes, it was a simple flash of light, drop in temperature, or a faint noise or smell. But there was the rare occasion when all senses came into play, and for an instant, the curtains of reality parted and a true experience played out. When any such moment occurred, there was the same sensation that spread across me. My hair follicles would tingle and stand on end as shivers spread across my skin. It felt like someone poured ice-cold water down my spine and through my body. My heart seemed to skip a few beats and grow louder, thump against my rib cage harder. Though I felt awash with fear, it wasn't actually fear that I felt— it was a melancholic fascination that I couldn't turn away from. A nagging sense of tragedy and beauty that I couldn't attain. Like the moth's fatal dance with the flame, like trying to grasp mercury with your fingers. Each experience made me hungry for the next. I became addicted.

I was in a small town outside Metamarie, Louisiana speaking with a group of locals at the farmer's market regarding some folklore in the surrounding areas. I had gathered enough information and had planned on moving on up to Philadelphia the next evening to investigate another cluster of potential sights. Most of the stories they told me I had heard or seen already, or they were too simple for me to follow up on. As I was wrapping up, one of the elder women said to me,
 "ain't seen nothing till you come across the *girl who burns....*"

I asked her what she meant, but her peers hushed her and said I shouldn't bother. I asked again, but they shut me down and began to look uncomfortable, shifting their feet along the ground, looking off and changing the subject. I let it go and thanked them for their time. I strolled through the market. I was walking off to ponder my notes when I saw the older lady from before waving me over across the street.

I looked around and walked briskly over. She stood next to an old and withered man sitting in a tattered lawn chair; he was obviously blind, with blacked out sunglasses and a white cane leaning against his leg. By his feet lay a sleeping bloodhound, the folds of his jowls spread on the sidewalk, a loud snore came from its open mouth.

"This here's my husband, Luther"... she told me "he seen that *Girl who burns*, he'll tell ya…even tell you where she is…. if you got the gumption to go…." She gently patted him on the shoulder and told him, "He's that old man I told you asking about all the ghosts... tell him about the Girl…" My curiosity drew me closer to the couple. This is where I heard the tale.

According to legend, there was a plantation that had fallen to ruins close to the Civil War. The Master of the plantation, Cornelius Baxter, was crippled with drink and insanity. He took it out on everyone around him. He had a wife, two sons, and a young daughter. Both of his sons were killed during the war, and his wife passed on shortly after, unable to live with her grief. After the war was over, and the confederacy had lost, Baxter was left with nothing. He and his young daughter, barely sixteen, were left alone in a dark and dilapidated antebellum home. It was on a night of such drunken depravity that old man Baxter snapped and had his way cruelly with his own daughter.

He kept his daughter as a prisoner in her own home. His mistreatment of her continued for weeks until, one night, at the pinnacle of his depravity, she managed to break free. This drove Baxter into a murderous rage as he chased her through the house. He caught her by her hair and dragged her into the grand room. He doused her in kerosene lamp oil and set her on fire. Coated in the thick combustive fuel, she burned alive. As she burned, the fire spread to the great carpets and curtains, consuming the furniture and tapestries. Eventually, the entire home was consumed.

Years swept by, and the storms called the marshes and swamps forth to claim the remains of the horrors of the Baxter estate. Only a handful of locals knew of the infamous legend, and only a smaller handful had seen the flickering of the flames that still burned around the home. Only a few heard the cries of the girl, wrapped in unholy fire, floating through the remains of the old place.

I had to see it for myself. I delayed my plans for the next evening, not knowing how far off the beaten path I was about to fall. I slept late into the next day and had a modest brunch of poached eggs, strawberries, and a side of crawfish cheese grits, a local dish I enjoyed immensely. I spent the early afternoon typing into my laptop all the notes from the past few days. I started a new folder in which I briefly input the tragedy of the Baxter daughter. I went to the farmer's market and crossed the street to where I had met the couple the day before. Luther was still there in his chair, the bloodhound still snoring by his feet.

Standing behind him was a young man with a boyish face, but with the immense body of a linebacker, and the cold stare of an angry man. Luther introduced the young man as his grandson. Luther told me he would drive me to where I needed to go.

It was a quiet ride down the dusty country roads in the old pick up truck, but it did not take long to reach our destination. These two gentlemen weren't as interested in idle conversation, though I imagined Luther told great tales. I respected their silence and concentrated on my surroundings. Out of the small downtown led a main road that curved left to a series of state roads that led out to the main highway. To the right of the main road eventually turned into a dirt road that led off into the backcountry where the road split into several smaller dirt paths that disappeared into thick foliage of trees and marsh areas. We were not even six miles down that dirt road before it split off. Luther's grandson slowed down.

Luther asked, "Where we at?" His grandson replied, "The busted fence by the swamp mouth…"

And then Luther turned to me smiling, "Now mister, you going to mention me in that book of yours?"

"Yes sir, it would be a pleasure to mention you and how much you helped me. It's the least I can do," I replied

"That's good to hear." His smile faded as his blind eyes stared off to the side of the road. "Listen carefully, as I don't want you to be getting lost and writing anything bad about me now. Right there, you see that old busted wooden post fence? Directly behind that is a footpath that leads off through the marsh and up through Sinful Swamp. 'Bout a hundred and some years ago, used to be the road up to the Ol' Baxter Place. About eighty or so years ago, they built a fence to keep folk out from the area. Folks tend to go crazy out there, marshes and swamps both bad places too. Don't call it Sinful for nothin'. But if you stay straight through the path, it'll lead you to the dry side o' the marsh. You'll see back there where the swamp swallowed up half of the old property. But part of it still stands— rooms, staircase, archways, and all. Vines and trees had their way too, but you can see how it used to be. In there, once the sun starts to set, you may get a chance to see her. You won't have to go in if you ain't inclined… if she shows, you'll know."

Nervously I asked, "By myself? Are you sure you can't come with me?"

"My grandson is wise enough to know he ain't got time to waste on the dead. As for myself," and then he turned again, smiling at me behind those old and blind eyes, "I've seen her before… You do as I said, you can't miss it. If for some reason you do, don't fret none…it will find you."

I climbed out of the pick up when he turned to me and said, "You got about three hours until it's black as pitch out here… I would be out of there way before that if I was you. My grandson will be back here after dinnertime, in about two and a half hours to pick you back up and take you back into town. Don't want nobody disappearing after following something Ol' Luther said… got a bad enough reputation as is. Bring this flashlight to help stay on that path I told you not to stray from… and you stop by tomorrow and talk to me 'fore you leave… understand?"

"Yes sir, and thank you for all you've done. How long do you propose it will take me to reach the remains?" I replied.

"Not so short you won't miss anything along the way, but not so long you can't get there and be back by the time my grandson is back to get you…"

I tried to lean in and thank his grandson, "And thank you especially for going out of your way to help me with transportation…"

Luther's grandson slowly turned his head toward me with eyes colder than the breeze in the air, his forehead etched in a permanent scowl. He said nothing, but gave a quick upward nod with his chin, I assumed it was recognition of sorts, though without Luther with us, I would have thought otherwise. And after a slow u-turn, the old pick up sped off down the road.

I stepped into the thick grassland and made my way toward the broken fence. On the other side, slightly parting the overgrown thicket of grass and wildflowers, I noticed the route Luther spoke of. I walked along the concealed path as the grassy field began to grow damp and disappeared into the shadow of the trees. The knees of cypress trees began to emerge as the marsh lands opened up. Inside was the hum of the locusts and the many chirps from the scattered choir of frogs. Dragonflies buzzed by my face. My hands frantically swatted mosquitoes that tried to land. I walked through the marshes, watching the sky between the branches. The sunlight had begun to cool and melt into an orange sherbet color. The trees grew denser. I saw cottonwoods and dogwoods bloom along the walls of pine. Tangles of wisteria and blackberry bushes. The swarms of gnats and mosquitoes grew thicker as the smell of the swamp began to fill the air. Amidst the gathering darkness, fireflies sparkled in twirling, blinking patterns. The scent was damp and dark, sulfurous from the escaping gases of rotten vegetation, but fresh and growing, alive and breathing. The sounds of unseen creatures began emerging from the undergrowth. As I began to grow closer to the edge of the swamp, the sky began to darken into the color of a red grapefruit swirled with streaks of amber. The day was coming to a close, as the shadows grew longer, pooling together along the ground. I walked a little faster, beginning to be concerned about my time.

Eventually, the beginning of the swamp came into my view, as well as the path that broke left and went along the perimeter. Remembering Luther's specific direction, I followed along the left. Surrounding the path, and as far as I could see, were enormous groves of ancient oak trees. They stood twenty to thirty feet with great giant branches, too heavy for upward growth, grew into and along the ground. The black waters of Sinful Swamp were covered in green ooze and littered with lily pads. Willows hung their weeping branches down as if praying to the secrets below. The adjacent side was obscured by shadows and growth. I could not see the remains. As I walked further around the swamp, I saw the corner foundation of what was once the Baxter Plantation, my heart skipped in excitement as I quickened my pace.

I came along the site rather quickly, and stopped to observe the scene. The back wall and portions of roof from where the mighty plantation once stood were still evident, though they were strangled with vines and moss. I could see that a good bit of the roof had fallen through the years and left much of the house exposed to the elements.

I could see a grand staircase that spiraled down in the left side of the house. At one point, the staircase must have led to the second floor of the house, but now it spiraled up into the branches of an oak tree. The masonry of the remaining walls, along with the marble of the columns and staircase glowed like bones in moonlight. I walked ever closer as the path of weeds led me directly to the front of the Baxter place.

What a remarkable building this must have been, but now it lay forgotten like the preserved bones of an ancient beast. I stepped up into its rib cage. The columns towering above me were entangled with kudzu. I noticed an old metal rocking chair rusting underneath a cover of wild jasmine vines. What would have been the great room was now a black hole opening into the swamp below. The walls were black with soot, mud, vines, and leaves. To my right was the darkness of the swamp and cypress trees growing through the remains of a wall. To my left was the grand staircase draped with the branches of an oak. I dared not step on the wooden boards in the living room for fear of falling. I simply stood up on the broken base of the front pillars and marveled at the passage of time. I heard the hum of the insects, the screeching of a bird flying away, and the rustle of the leaves in the cool evening breeze. Then I heard *Her*.

Nature grew quiet as, somewhere over in the darkened corner, a soft whimpering began. It sounded like the wounded whimpering of a young woman, but hollowed and old, as if it came from a century of anguish. It was close to me. I could feel the whimpers as they became louder. I could feel the temperature drop. As her sullen cries became louder still, that familiar feeling spread through me. My hairs stood on end and that ice-water sensation poured down my scalp and spine. There was unquestionably some spirit making itself known no more than twenty feet in front of me, to the left of the staircase, hidden in the darkness. I was frozen as her tortured weeping rose and fell. The atmosphere around me began to feel desolate and deranged, hopeless and hurtful. I could feel her suffering.

This had never happened. I have felt sympathy for the poor souls I have been able to witness and, of course, I feel remorse for the horrible happenings for the victims, but never had I been awash with what they might have been actually feeling. It began to affect me deeply, it slipped down to my soul and called forth recognition and empathy. My heart filled with cold, cold fear. Not fear for myself or my health, but the fear of being lost, the fear of being betrayed.

Tears blurred my sight. The darkness reeled while I soaked in the misery. Her weeping rose again and then fell quiet. I strained my eyes to peer into the nest of shadows where her spirit hid. I could see nothing. I moved to take a step. Gravel bounced to the concrete steps, breaking the silence. Her words were cold and clear *"Leave… Me….Alone..."*

> **" It was a soul wrenching, horrible scream. I gasped at the pure raw suffering being emitted through the air.**

Her voice was soft, yet stone, it was not of this earth and it pierced me like a needle. At the end of the word *"Alone,"* her voice trailed off into a long and woeful wail. The unearthly moan gradually grew louder into a frightful wail. The terror seized me again. In the darkness, I saw her flames beginning to flicker.

It was a thin line of flames that began, light orange in color that outlined her face and neck, and then spread down gently revealing her shoulders and torso, arms and legs. I could see the faint outline of the 1800's style dress, lace, ribbons, and all. Her inner features and form were still masked by the dark. Her moaning quieted for a moment to where I could hear the gentle lapping of the ethereal flames. The thin glowing lines began to die down like decreasing the flame of a gas grill. I began to lose sight of her form. Desperately, I began to stammer out. "But no… wait I haven't…."

Then she screamed.

It was a soul wrenching, horrible scream. I gasped at the pure raw suffering being emitted through the air. It felt as though electricity ran through my veins. The sensation was overwhelming. I could see the outline of her face with her mouth stretched unnaturally open. It was then that she burst into full roaring flames. The light was brilliant, startling and magnificent. I could clearly see her entire form now, including her outdated dress. The flames that radiated from her were indescribably beautiful. Staring at them, I felt perhaps what the first humans felt sitting around a fire as their old gods materialized before them.

I stood awestruck. Their colors likened to shades of burning oranges, bleeding reds, and searing yellows, but unlike any earthly colors I had seen before. And though they cast off such light, it was self-contained in that it seemed to come from within her. She cast off dreadful, twisting shadows all around her from the staircase, from the overhanging branches of the giant oak, from the thick Spanish moss that draped down like velvet curtains. The flames and her seemed eerily animated, as if an old film of the past was being transposed against her figure.

I could hear the stomping of heavy feet and the slamming of weighty doors. I saw the outline of shackles around her wrist as her scream softened to a series of sobs. She was underneath the stairwell, her body turned three quarters away from me. She slowly turned her head in my direction. Her head craned too far over her shoulder, abnormally glancing at me. For a moment, I noticed how attractive her facial features were, the feminine curve of her jaw and nose, rich full lips, and gorgeous round staring eyes. She was remarkably beautiful— until she opened her mouth.

She screamed again, her fires alive, growing brighter this time. I could see her clothes catch flame, her hair burning and melting into a black mass, the skin of her face and arms bubbling up into agonizing blisters popping and oozing down. Her eyes continued to stare as they boiled in their sockets and ran like raw egg down her face, her open mouth dripping liquefying lips.. I watched the skin from her arms sizzle and fall off of the bone. She jumped to her feet and ran in the circles through the remains of the house. The flames of her ectoplasmic fire flapped like the wings of a horrible angel. She fell to her knees again, the screaming fading back into pitiful weeping. Then she began another transformation.

Gradually, her flesh and features began to reform themselves and the flames seemed to knit back her clothing. She straightened her back up and began humming. Softly, gently she hummed, and softly sang the chorus of some hauntingly, achingly elegant song. The flames around her began to soften and alter into a deep peculiar violet or phosphorescent purple. She stood to her feet humming this sad and lovely sound. She glanced up to me for a brief second and turned, walking forlornly toward the staircase. I could hear her still as she began to ascend, one step at a time. I wanted to rush over and take her into my arms, comfort her, and try to wash the pain away. Time froze in this moment as she ascended further through the branches of the oak, her light flickering from within its leaves until finally it was no more and she was truly gone.

The air seemed to grow balmier. The sounds of the bullfrogs and owls, the buzz of the millioned winged insect came back to my ears. The electrical sensation faded. I began to breathe again, deeper breaths. I noticed the battalion of constellations shining above me. The glow from the moon rising up above the trees. I had no idea how long my experience had been, how long I had stood here on this marble block, my hand resting on this vine choked pillar.

I shook my head and tried to focus my mind. Luther's Grandson! My ride into Town! I hopped down and ran back to the path, jogging all the way around the edge of the swamp, tripping along the roots and vines. My mind was numb. I could only move forward, focusing down on the path as thin limbs scratched my face and the top of my head. I stumbled into the soft earth a few times, but got back up still jogging, out of breath. I made it to the marshes where I tripped across the cypress knees and splashed black mud up my trousers and soaked my shoes. My glasses bent as my face hit the ground. I ran on, no telling for how long, underneath the canopy of trees and the darkness of night until I could see the clearing up ahead that led out into the field and back to the road. I ran now, ignoring the burning of my old legs, and the tightening of my chest until I was out into the field. I took great gasping breaths and then realized I was weeping.

I was a mess. My face was tear streaked and bloodied from tiny scratches, my clothes were torn and muddied, and I was more emotional than I had ever been. More exhausted too. As I reached the broken fence, two headlights turned onto the dirt road a few miles up. They rose brighter into sight and sped past me, sending a shower of gravel and dirt against my legs and chest. The automobile turned around racing back to where I was standing. I darted back toward the trees until I recognized the old pickup. I smiled but was met with a scowl as the truck's brakes squealed to a stop. It was Luther's grandson and three of his friends all as big as him piled up front. His unfriendly gaze seemed a welcome sight. "Thank you so much for coming..." I spit out.

He cut me off... "YOU are late, man... Only came back so I won't get in trouble with PawPaw. An' I won't be getting in trouble because some fool gets himself killed. You will ride in the back now..."

"Thank you very much." I had to say again. He simply stared at me along with his other friends. They must have all practiced together, for each of their gazes were equally unfriendly. I climbed into the back and we sped off. I slid around a bit, which was met by great laughter coming from inside the cab. I stared back at the passing road and the shadowy trees. I tried to get my head together, to recount every detail. I tried to decide what angle to tell in my book. I tried to focus on the days ahead, the things to do. But all I could think about was Her.

I stay awake all-night thinking of how enraptured I was. I felt like a child in love. The one meeting wasn't enough. I needed more. I admit now, I was not thinking rationally at all. I felt obsessed, nearly driven mad with desire to capture or embrace this... exquisite creature.

For the first time in my life, I believe I felt the pangs of love. All I felt was the desire to be around one single soul. I should have sensed I was losing control. I should've known I was crossing into a realm that would be hard to return from. I plunged headlong into oblivion anyway.

I rushed to the food market again, remembering where I came across Mrs. Primrose, a lady who knew a lot about the dark arts. When I reached her, I asked to look at some of the old books, hear some of the old spells. I inquired about supplies and tools, reassuring her that it was all for a chapter in my book and, though I would pay greatly, they were merely in the interest of my studies. She warned me against using such things, unless I was absolutely sure I understood the gravity of the situation. Based on two different spells, I gathered together a list of ghastly items: bundles of bones, strings of teeth, a black vial of thick liquid, precious stones, rare herbs, jagged pieces of a divining mirror, and long black candles tied together by twists of matted hair. I placed them all gently in a long box I purchased made from the boards of a coffin. I paid her for her services, lessons, and time before making my exit. I rushed through the isles and tried to get to the street when I heard Luther call my name. I turned and went toward him.

He smiled, the sunlight bouncing off his sunglasses. "Hey there... heard you was wandering around here still...Well? Did you have any luck last night?"

I felt a silent rage in me at the questioning, but I tried to push it aside. "Yes... very interesting...it was quite a sight... I will definitely mention it in my upcoming book. I will also make sure to thank you for all your help...."

"That all.... Hmmmmnph ...figured on a bigger reaction than that...." And then he began to sniff the air around me, leaning in closer to the box I clutched in my arms. "What's that I smell... smell like.... nightshade... and burned up cloth, some kinda oils... you haven't been shopping 'round Miss Primrose by chance?"

"Who, no, these are items for research...." But he cut me off....

"Beause I heard you spent a good bit with her not too long ago.. Everybody tells Ol' Luther what's going on... I gots eyes everywhere.... You say what you want to, but you listen close to this old man's words Doctor, don't be fooling around with nothing you don't understand...."

I had heard enough, I apologized and tried to excuse myself quickly.

"I told you I had seen her before, remember?" That statement stopped me and I turned back toward him.

"Yeah... I seen her too.... I know that she is more than 'very interesting'.... I know about the colors and how pretty she sings....I know how much it can be to a man that thinks he knows a lot... I fell in love with her once, long time ago... went completely crazy too 'cause of it.... Cut my own eyes out with a straight razor and ended up in the mental hospital...." He leaned forward and slid his glasses toward the end of his nose, revealing the scarred, carved out sockets of his skull that once were his eyes. The skin was like jagged, but soft worn leather. Nausea curled in my belly, one of disgust and ultimately, fear for myself. He continued. "I went mad wild wanting to see those colors again, to hold her, to contain her like lightning bugs in a mason jar. I knew in my soul it was wrong, which is why I did what I did, which is why my mind shut itself off before it did damage to the rest of me."

He pushed the glasses back and smiled again, "But I got better... found the Lord and my wife.... Got a family... Now I see better than I ever did before...That was when I was a young man and could afford a few years of healing...A man like you ought not risk it this late in the game... An' I can see that you seem to be a different man than yesterday afternoon.... You should heed these words from one old man ... to another old man."

Part of me deep down did heed his words, and a glimmer of recognition began to surface. This desire uncharacteristically threatened my reasoning. I thought of my life and my career. I missed my bedroom and my fireplace. I missed sipping tea and reading. Missed the comfort of solace and writing a new book, simply, one word at a time. I wanted to go home. I felt tired, very tired.

But then a surge passed through me as I recalled those violet petals of fire, those woeful eyes, that haunting song. I had never felt such passion toward anything besides knowledge, and even knowledge didn't enlighten my heart the way she did. I was lost and drifting into myself. "You are right," I told him, placing my hand on his shoulder with reassurance, "I'm a little tired from all this traveling. I need to get home and get to work finishing this book. Thank you for all you have done for me. I really need to get back." And I rushed off down the street. I glanced back to see him leaning on his cane, looking in my direction, perhaps listening to my scuffling feet pass away. He was not smiling. He simply shook his head.

I went back to my room and paid for an additional night. I rearranged my flight plans to a route via Amtrak train and made arrangements for my boarding. I contacted the school I was scheduled to visit in two days to inform them of my exciting discovery. I canceled my other stops in other cities, as I had gathered all the information I needed. I gathered together all of my supplies in a knapsack and called for a taxi. The Gypsy Rose Taxi service arrived within fifteen minutes and I asked the driver to take me toward the edge of the city.

I had remembered the first turn correctly, but was craning my neck looking for the broken fence. Eventually we came upon it and I paid the man his fare. I told him there would be twice the amount if he would pick me up sometime around noon tomorrow, nearly twenty hours from when he dropped me off. He agreed, but looked at me as though I was completely crazy. Which, at the time, would have been a fair assumption.

I tumbled out of the car with my knapsack loaded heading back to the path down to Sinful Swamp. I remembered the path as it lay before me. The swarms of insects thickened as sweat began to dampen my brow. I approached the mouth of the swamp, the knees of cypress trees like rows of serrated teeth. I walked faster alongside them. My heart beat faster as I worked my way around the bend. The remains of the dreadful place came into view once again.

I stood under the towering columns. Under the squish of my shoe was the molded remnants of carpet, now mottled with mushrooms. I found a clearing approximately ten feet from where she had shown herself the night before. I then went to work like a young man unleashed, reading through the brittle pages and placing the items and totems in a specific pattern. I marked out a perfect circle, measuring a four-foot circumfer- ence, and drew out the five intersecting lines of a pentagram web inside. I read through the incantations and instructions. I attempted two spells at once. It was a simple divination spell and a simple holding spell. I planned to improvise anything else that followed. After everything was set and checked for the fourth time, all I had to do was wait.

I went and sat on a fallen pillar and looked out into the swamp. The head and limbs of Grecian Statues that once greeted guests on the front lawns of the Baxter Plantation, now barely stood above the water line, their fac- es and arms covered with moldy green slime. A crane swooped through, disappearing under the hanging branches. The day's bright light softened and filled with orange and gold. Mosquitoes fed from my skin, but I sim- ply watched them take their share. I did not care.

When nighttime surrounded me, I stepped a little closer toward the en- trance. Still no sound to be heard. I walked up on the creaking floorboards again and attempted to light the candles at the top and bottom of the circle. I poured the vial's black and putrid liquid along the intersecting lines within. I spoke the written lines out into the quiet of the night. I then could not help but take a look at myself and the spectacle I had be- come. How my colleagues would laugh at how far I'd fallen— either that or they'd want to commit me. I sighed, gathered my senses, and then felt Her enter the room.

The same electrical surge pulsated through me, sending shivers along my skin. My heart beat faster and the air grew colder than the natural night. I heard Her whisper, *"Please don't...Go away... Leave me... alone... no..."* She floated around me, invisible, but present. The cool wind blew as nature quieted on her arrival. I heard the whimpering again, the piti- ful weeping, the painful low moans. Sensations swam through me. I was overcome with Her emotions, once again drawn into her exquisite misery. She passed around me, making me swoon and I tried to be careful with my step so as not to fall through the hole in the floorboards. She rushed past me again and stopped somewhere beneath the staircase. I gathered that this must have been where she was kept during those fateful weeks. Her weeping quieted again as I repeated the incantation.

At the last line of words, she ripped into another soul-wrenching scream, so intense I fell down and braced myself on one knee. She burst into eerie, ghostly flames and I was mesmerized by their glow. She rushed toward me screaming, the mad ethereal fire flapping wildly about her beautiful face. She passed through me with a grave and abysmal chill. I sat in horror and fascination as she blazed by me and through me.

I tried to reach her. "Please stop for a moment... it's okay... no one is going to hurt you... I think you are ... truly beautiful..."

And she stopped screaming to turn and look at me. She stared into my face, and the flames around Her softened their fiery tones and gradually changed to cooler colors. She opened and closed her mouth as if she was speaking, but I heard no words. And then it hit me. The song she was singing last night... "Once was lost... now I'm found..." It was Amazing Grace. I began to hum the chorus and she looked at me in vague interest. She began to hum along with me after a moment, her flames now the soothing moonbeam blue and purple again. She walked closer toward the circle I had made, tiny flames drifted behind in her step. I began the second incantation.

A moment of fear passed over both of us as she realized some force was pulling her to the center. She stopped the song in Her mind and began begging to be left alone. Ignoring feelings of doubt, I pushed on further, releasing the herbs and repeating the words. She began to weep again uncontrollably and the flames towered above her angry and orange, fearful and red. I shouted the final sentence again, as her screams grew louder and louder. She tried to turn and run but was held back by something she didn't understand. She thrashed about within the perimeter of the lines I had drawn, but could not break free.

My making had trapped her. She wailed horribly, her flames towering wildly against the branches and the moss, but not burning anything but her. I watched in morbid fascination as she melted and burned before me and became whole again. She railed against my invisible walls and looked at me with wounded eyes. I stared back at them as they bubbled and melted before me and pooled back into their former state. I began to hum Amazing Grace, and, after a while, it calmed her. She began to hum it on her own, causing her flames to mellow as well. I watched her all through the night singing so softly to herself, smoldering in her own flames. I watched her as the pink sun began to rise and she slowly faded with the morning light, an occasional flame dancing inside the circle.

Carefully I took a knife and cut outside the circle's perimeter down through the moss and mold, into the old carpet. I cautiously removed the stones and bones away and gingerly rolled the damp cloth that once held her. I placed the carpet into the keeping box I bought and set the items on top, closing and sealing the lid. I then took the knife and pierced my finger causing blood to trickle down to be caught in the vial. Like a thief, I gathered my things and climbed out of the place and back onto the path. I walked briskly back once again.

I was too consumed with the night behind me and the nights that lay before me to even notice the path. Quickly I ambled out of the swamp and through the marsh. The taxi driver from the night before waited for me. I told him to take me to the train station and paid him too much. The journey home was a blur and I found myself back in my own house in front of my own fireplace. I crouched down in front and carefully opened the box. The smell of Sinful Swamp filled the room. I replaced all the totems back in their original order and poured my blood onto the intersecting lines and waited for nightfall to say the words again.

That was two weeks ago, possibly, though I barely notice the time at all these days. All I do is wait for the night to fall and for my beloved to reveal herself to me. It took her quite a bit of coaxing, but she could not escape the web I spun for her. And, as I said from the beginning, I may have done a terrible thing by stealing her from her home, or by not trying to free her soul, but it's really not that way. I have rescued her by bringing her here and bonding her to my blood and my circle. She no longer melts or bleeds, her skin no longer seems to blister or boil. She doesn't wail or moan or beg to be left alone. She didn't want to be alone; no one truly does in the end.

I have learned so much from her. I realize now that my entire quest was meant to lead me to her. I understand her and why she burns. She burns because of the horrible tragedy and immense fear and pain that was inflicted upon a little girl a long, long time ago. She burned throughout the years to be remembered, to call out into a world that let this happen, or, perhaps, to get the attention of the gods who looked the other way while it occurred. And now, She Who Burns, burns for me. Her flames have consumed me.

The phone rang so much I had ripped it from the wall. My answering machine was so loaded with messages that it stopped taking them. It was ripped from the wall also. They all want to see my big secret, but I'll never show them, no one will see her but me, as long as I can help it. I have boarded up all the windows and doors and have unplugged the television and computer. I haven't eaten, drank, or slept since my return. My wrinkled frame has grown weaker. Two of my front teeth fell out into my hands when I yawned earlier today doesn't. It matters not.

I am not the man I was twenty years ago, not the man I was two weeks ago either. I grow weaker and more tired with every passing hour. Grow more and more feeble as I try to do anything but stand guard over my girl. Soon I will be crossing over to that theatre beyond reality and I will have my chance to shine in the night alongside my beloved. And the world and all who knew me will see that I did not cast it all aside for academia. I did not miss out on the passions of life or its vital forces. I found what the great artists wrote stories, sonnets, and poems about. In the end I didn't miss out on anything but more time.

"Amazing Grace, how sweet the sound that saved a wretch like me
I once was lost but now I am found, was blind but now I see
Was blind but now I see"

A FEW FEET FROM NORMALCY

BY JOSHUA MAHN

You can really do anything!

I mean it! You can try to do anything. You can do so much more than you ever thought you could.

You should never, ever feel powerless. I did, once, but no more! Not anymore!

You can do anything!
You should try everything!

In life, there are so many people trying to tell you what you can and cannot do.

Aren't you curious about something? Anything? Go on. Please. Think for a moment about something you've been dying to try, but have been scared of what people will think.

Free yourself from that. Close your eyes. Let the river of life wash that shame away.

Now open them. You feel better already— I see it!

Life belongs to those who try.

~~~

All of life is stuck in these "grooves", see, and all you ever need to do is shift yourself out of that groove by a few feet, and everything will change. Pick a new place, and walk to it. Try something new on the menu. Talk to a stranger. Follow a new friend. Go ahead and have another coffee. We only have our boredom to lose.
~~~

One day, just after work, I drove. I just drove. I didn't drive home, I didn't tell my family. I just drove and drove and drove. I didn't pay attention— maybe I even drove in circles, but it doesn't even matter. I just got myself good and lost. This was my first real taste of freedom. When was the last time you did something just for you? I mean truly. Not giving yourself five minutes before you do something for another person, I mean thinking exclusively, solely, for you. It's not selfish— it's natural.

I became hooked immediately. What a rush! Just driving while the phone rang and rang and rang. I had to taste more. I drove on the wrong side of the road for a while. I had never been brave enough to do that before. I was always scared someone would call the police. People honked. Boy, were they mad! But nobody actually did anything about it. Can you believe that?

I finally pulled my car over when it was just about out of gas, I rolled into a supermarket parking lot, and I ambled out. I left my phone in the seat, keys in the ignition, and just looked around. There are so many things, I realized, that I had never even given myself permission to try.

I pushed the shopping carts out of their corral, and I walked to the back of the market. I played in the dumpster, and burrowed to the bottom. I opened some bags to see what was inside. I climbed into the hedges. The branches scratched me but it was a good sting. By now, the sun was setting and I was getting bored, so I walked in ever-broadening loops.

Then, I saw the most incredible thing. You wouldn't believe me if you couldn't see it here! Right there, in the storm drain, was a huge clump of the most beautiful blonde hair.

It was sopping wet, but still perfectly good. I knew the wig was for me because I've always wanted long, blonde hair. It was so gorgeous. I picked it up and put it on and it was so right. Because I've always wanted it.

~~~

Maybe it was Tengri. That's who Genghis Khan worshipped, I hear. I heard if you're doing good it's because he's rewarding you, and if you're doing bad, it's because he's punishing you and that's that. Maybe! Old Genghis seemed to go against the grain and try whatever he wanted, and he did great. He built an empire this way!

Maybe I'm the demiurge. I'm not god but maybe I'm what's just underneath.

Anyway.

~~~

After picking my hair out of the drain, I realized that I have never, ever been in the sewers. I tried to lift the grate but it was too heavy. My hands were bleeding pretty badly, so I had to stop. But I followed my gut to where I thought it let out, and I was so right! I crawled and I wiggled and I squirmed, but soon enough I was sitting there under the storm grate, just a few feet beneath normalcy, but in a world so new and incredible! There were mosses and growths I had never seen in my life. I chewed on the cigarette butts down there and I think I got a good nicotine buzz. A whole family parked and went to go shopping and even stood right above me, right over my head! They had no clue, they had no idea. I wanted to laugh so badly, but I knew they wouldn't get the joke. I let them walk away and that was the end of that I guess. They'll never know— they didn't let themselves look down there.

After that, it started to rain.

Have you ever just sat in the rain?
I mean, sat there?

Most people say they don't like the rain. They run from it. But why?

What has it done? It won't hurt you, not really. You hurt you. The water flowed over me and brought me paper bags and cigarette butts and hamburger buns and water bottles. I was bathed in the world and it tasted so sweet to my lips. I drank the stream until my body could take it no more, and I let it loose back into the world, but that was okay too.


~~~
~~~~
~~~

I saw myself down there, you know.

I had been down there a few days by now. It was so much fun.

I heard a lot down there. I heard people arguing. I heard kids playing. I heard the police! They found my car. They were looking for me! My wife— she must be so confused! I laughed and I laughed. The world brought me food and it brought me water and it brought me toys. I knew I'd want to leave here before long, but, for now, I was so happy— so secure, so warm, so safe! It was so much fun sitting right under the parking lot, just being there, just being happy.


~~~
~~~~
~~~

I found myself down there, you know.

There he was.

I was crawling through my usual tunnel, doing some exploring. I looked so good. I could see my new wig, my tattered work pants, my raw belly, everything. He was eating something. I snuck up behind him, and, on account of I wasn't expecting anyone with me in my tunnel, he had no clue and I grabbed his throat and hit his head on the slick concrete again and again and he clawed my eye up real good which is why it's all swollen and pussy now. See this yellow stuff? But I hit him again and again until I died and here I am!

In the tunnels you can do anything.

~~~

Life belongs to those who try! You're the 'who' who tells you no!

I didn't need to buy anything new. I just had to stop letting the external world distract me. Imagine changing your whole world without a purchase, and as simply as not purchasing anything!

> **" Now, the woods were always a spooky place at night for me. But have I ever been eaten by an animal? No, of course not! Don't be ridiculous.**

Anyway.

A day or two after I killed myself, I remembered a strange fancy I had as a child.

I waited until a pickup truck parked near my tunnel, and when the driver went inside to shop, I crawled into the bed and waited.
When the lady was done with her shopping, I laid straight back, stiff as a board, and quiet as a mouse, and made believe I was on a rocket ship!

She drove so fast, I really believed I was on my way to mars, or something!

When she parked, I just stayed right there for a little bit, enjoying the feeling of the nice cool evening sun rays on my scabbed belly. I even took a little nap.
~~~

When I was done, it must have been really late at night, but I was refreshed.

I got up and looked around, and boy, did she ever live out in the boonies! What's funny is, out there, people are more scared of abstract notions like the weather or the government than they are of folks. She locked her doors, but she didn't even bother closing her windows all the way!

I went in and just looked around for a bit. I guess she was asleep, but that was alright. She had a cat and I cuddled it for a little bit, and then I fixed myself a little bit of a snack.

And you know what? For years and years, I told myself I wasn't supposed to drink grape soda, and for what? To impress someone? For my health? Well, if it's for me, then I'm at the wheel!

Anyway. I had a cheese sandwich and some soda and then I had a nice shower. I tried a little raw hamburger meat for the first time, and it tasted just like a good steak!

I moved some of her furniture around to give her a nice little surprise, and then I went out the way I came in.

Now, the woods were always a spooky place at night for me. But have I ever been eaten by an animal? No, of course not! Don't be ridiculous.

Stop.

I just walked and walked in the darkness and nothing attacked me at all. My new hair got caught on a branch or two, but I think that it still looks okay. I walked around and yelled- truly yelled, unhindered by fear of worrying some old worrywort- until my voice ran out. That felt really good. By the time I was done, I could see a road up ahead, and I followed it back this way and that. I took some naps, and I ate some weird things that looked nice. I caught a lizard and it wriggled. I swallowed a smooth pebble, and I loved that. I don't know how many times in my life I stopped myself from doing that, but I'm glad I did, now. I'm really hoping to find some smooth marbles before I'm done. Until then, I've been carrying some pennies and quarters in my cheeks, and I like that tang a lot. It reminds me of nosebleeds, but in a good way.

Anyway. I'm getting a little dizzy and I think I'm gonna try something really, really weird in a minute here, so I need to focus. But I just want to let you know that I love you so much, and that life belongs to the tryers. You have to give yourself permission. You have to say yes, and you have to know that those who don't try don't know what they're missing.

You deserve this.
You earn it just by trying. Go ahead. I know I will.